The rumblings of thunder and steady drumbeat of rain against the pavement must have masked the sound of an engine starting.

But there was no mistaking the squeal of tires fighting for traction as a car rounded the end of the aisle and raced toward them. "Gray?"

For a split-second, she flashed back to the sounds of Noah's truck racing up in her rearview mirror, ramming her car and spinning her over the railing of the bridge. Her breath lodged in her chest, and she couldn't seem to move. The bright beam of headlights blinded her.

"Allie!"

A vise clamped around her waist and she was off her feet, flying backward, out of the path of the car bearing down on her. In a span of milliseconds, she realized the lights kept her from seeing the driver's face. She felt the breeze of the car rushing past.

To the good people of Lee's Summit, Missouri, who were so kind, helpful and supportive of my hubby and me when our moving truck was broken into, and we got stranded there, waiting for repairs. Special shout-outs to the managers and staff at the Fairfield Inn for helping us clean up the mess and letting us hang out; to Officer Geno of the LSMO police department, who made us feel safe, guided us through the reporting process and even offered some of her police buddies to help us unload the truck; and to Jake at Lines & Designs Tattoos/Barber/UHaul rentals who was charming and helpful and had a thriving business (btw, if you need a haircut or tattoo, check him out!) who got on the phone and made things happen. Thank you.

THE EVIDENCE NEXT DOOR

USA TODAY Bestselling Author

JULIE MILLER

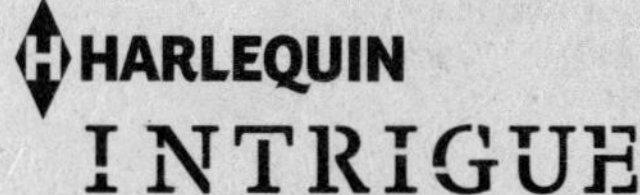

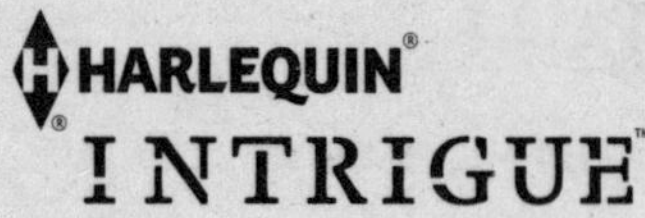

Recycling programs for this product may not exist in your area.

ISBN-13: 978-1-335-58273-7

The Evidence Next Door

For questions and comments about the quality of this book, please contact us at CustomerService@Harlequin.com.

Harlequin Enterprises ULC
22 Adelaide St. West, 41st Floor
Toronto, Ontario M5H 4E3, Canada
www.Harlequin.com

Printed in U.S.A.

Julie Miller is an award-winning *USA TODAY* bestselling author of breathtaking romantic suspense—with a National Readers' Choice Award and a Daphne du Maurier Award, among other prizes. She has also earned an *RT Book Reviews* Career Achievement Award. For a complete list of her books, monthly newsletter and more, go to juliemiller.org.

Books by Julie Miller

Harlequin Intrigue

Kansas City Crime Lab

K-9 Patrol
Decoding the Truth
The Evidence Next Door

The Taylor Clan: Firehouse 13

Crime Scene Cover-Up
Dead Man District

The Precinct

Beauty and the Badge
Takedown
KCPD Protector
Crossfire Christmas
Military Grade Mistletoe
Kansas City Cop

Rescued by the Marine
Do-or-Die Bridesmaid
Personal Protection
Target on Her Back
K-9 Protector
A Stranger on Her Doorstep

Visit the Author Profile page at Harlequin.com.

CAST OF CHARACTERS

Grayson Malone—Blood expert at the KCPD Crime Lab. Two prosthetic legs won't stop this disabled former Marine from getting a job done in the lab. He turned in his rifle and military training for a CSI kit two years ago. When a stalker targets his next-door neighbor, he's willing to be the criminalist who solves the crime—but can he be the man she needs to keep her safe?

Allie Tate—A veteran herself, Allie is an independent woman who won't take any guff from a stubborn patient or a grumpy Marine Corps veteran. But when the nightmare that ended her Navy career and forced her to relocate to Kansas City resurrects itself in a bloody campaign of psychological terror, she turns to the reluctant hero next door to save both her sanity and her life.

Noah Boggs—Allie's ex-boyfriend now in military prison.

Doug Friesen—A coworker at the physical therapy clinic.

Ben Hunter—Another patient at the physical therapy clinic.

Ivy Burroughs—She's always matchmaking.

Bubba Summerfield—The superintendent at Grayson and Allie's apartment building.

Prologue

Three months earlier

The visitor waited patiently until the prisoner was shown into the room. It wasn't the first prison the visitor had been to, and though the age of the building and the uniforms might be different, it was still a prison. The blank expression on the prisoner's face, carefully revealing nothing but hatred and distrust, was familiar, too.

Although it was an accepted rule that the inmate remain handcuffed during the interview, the visitor refused the guard's offer to chain him to the table, as well. "I'm looking for cooperation, not to make his stay here any more miserable than it already is."

"You know what he's in here for, don't you?"

The visitor nodded before waving the guard away. "I've done my homework. You may go."

"Your call." The guard shrugged, as though he didn't think that was the best choice. But the visitor wanted something very specific from the man sitting across the table, and that wasn't going to happen if a guard who was armed and wearing a flak vest hovered over them. "I'll be right outside that door. Watching. You got ten minutes."

The visitor didn't bother thanking the guard as the door closed and locked behind him. The prisoner didn't bother with introductions and niceties, either. "Cooperation? Who are you? My new attorney?"

The visitor studied the man's shaved head and brown eyes. In another world, he would probably be considered handsome. But rage, frustration and a focus on surviving versus the opportunity to settle into a successful, free life had given him hard edges. It had taken a while to find this man, and the visitor was counting on them sharing a need for retribution. "I can't offer you legal absolution. But I can offer you something you might find eminently satisfying."

"All I want is to get out of this place. I intend to keep my nose clean so I don't get any time tacked on to my sentence."

"You won't have to lift a finger and jeopardize your time here. I just have a question for you."

"I'm no snitch, either. I intend to stay in one piece until I do get out of here."

"There won't be a sign painted on your back, Mr. Boggs."

Boggs puffed up, wanting to correct the *Mister* appellation. But perhaps the skills from his mandated anger management class had kicked in—or maybe he was simply curious enough to know why a stranger had come to see him. He dropped his cuffed wrists onto the table and leaned forward. "Then what the hell do you want from me?"

The visitor set a photograph on the table and pointed to the image. "I want you to tell me everything you can about this woman."

Chapter One

Today

"Your arms and shoulders are too big."

Grayson Malone wobbled over the prostheses attached just above each knee and grabbed the balance bars on either side of him to steady himself. He'd made it up and down the rehabilitation center's ten-foot walkway all by himself, thank you very much, before the physical therapist with the long, honey-blond ponytail stepped up beside the railing. She crossed her arms and smirked up at him as if she was challenging him to prove her wrong.

"Too big?" He looked down into her gray-blue eyes and arched an eyebrow to meet her smirk. "They fit inside my T-shirt okay."

"Very funny."

Like him, Allison Tate was a veteran integrating back into the civilian world in Kansas City, Missouri. Although they'd served in different branches of the military, in different parts of the world, and in different capacities, he seemed to have more in common with her than any of the other therapists he worked with here at the clinic. Shared commiserations, pride and a sense of duty gave them plenty to talk about—as did the fact that they both lived in the same apartment building where veterans got a bit of a break on the monthly rent as a benefit of their service. In fact, they lived on the same floor, and had had several opportunities to connect outside of PT over the past few months. She was easy to talk to, and she was a good physical therapist. Allie knew when to push him and when to pull back as he adjusted to life in a wheelchair or walking on his new prosthetic limbs.

She was pushing now. "Seriously, Gray, the reason you're back here for PT is because you've pushed your recovery too hard. Yes, we finally have your new prostheses adjusted to fit the changing musculature of your thighs, which should even out your gait. But you're going to keep getting those spasms in your back and hips if you don't give your body a chance to adapt. You've been doing more than your PT exercises when you work out at home, haven't you?" she challenged.

"I was in the Marines for eleven years, Allie. I'm used to working out every day." He lifted his leg another shaky step and continued down the walkway. If he walked slowly enough and concentrated, he didn't need the rails, his crutches or the damn chair to be mobile. Although his wheelchair was still his fastest mode of travel, and his go-to when he needed to rest his back or give his residual limbs a break.

"There's a difference between being physically fit and having too much muscle." She moved along beside him. "You're top-heavy. It's throwing your balance off. Plus, it's more weight to carry on those joints." She flattened her palms at either side of his waist to steady him as he turned, and the skin beneath his T-shirt leaped at even that impersonal touch. "You need to take dancing lessons, relearn where your center of gravity is."

"Dancing?" Gray chuckled, chasing her down in swaying slow motion as she backed along the railing. He was fourth-generation military, a man's man. At least, he used to be. He wasn't sure exactly where he qualified on the macho scale now. He hadn't been man enough to keep his ex-girlfriend after shipping home on a medical discharge. Brittany had barely been able to look at him below his chin, much less help with his recovery. Despite her teary apology and professions of love, she'd confessed that lying in bed beside a man with no feet "*freaked her out*" and she'd broken up with him. Now he qualified for geekdom as a chemist and blood analyst for the Kansas City Crime Lab. Not exactly the catch he used to be. "I don't think I'm exactly the ballet or ballroom type."

Allie ducked beneath the railing and planted herself in front of him, forcing him to grab the railing to stop himself from plowing into her with his forward momentum. Instead of backing up to avoid a collision, Allie took a half step toward him. She braced one hand on the waistband of his sweatpants and splayed the other at the center of his chest. "Overworking one part of your body at the expense of another skews your balance. Dancing helps with coordination and mobility, too." She nudged his chest back, squaring his weight over his hips before sliding her hand up to his shoulder. Then she pried his left hand off the bar and rested her fingers lightly in his palm. "Put your other hand at my waist," she instructed.

Gray hated that he had to squeeze her arm for a moment until he found his balance over what used to be his legs and settled his hand above the flare of her hip. "Like this?"

"There you go. Let's hold this position for sixty seconds. You're a tall guy. Own it. Get used to the feel of your upper body centered over your hips, not leaning forward on your crutches or the bar. I want your legs and core to do the work, not your arms." She adjusted her own stance, moving closer so that he had to hold the posture or risk toppling over onto her. "That's it."

As they stood there in the mockery of a ballroom dance pose, with Gray tightening his core muscles and keeping his shoulders back like a good Marine, he breathed in Allie's scent—a blend of something antiseptic, likely her hand gel, with something flowery and more intimate underneath. He wondered at the hints of femininity beneath her tallish, tomboy facade. She was always confident and strong. Sure, her pink scrubs and thick, gorgeous hair reminded him that she was a woman. And like the women he'd served with or who worked with him at KCPD, she was a pal—a valued, respected colleague. Before holding her in his arms and standing close enough for the heat of her thighs to reach his, he'd never realized Allison Tate was also a girlie girl.

She squeezed her hand in his and retreated a step, urging him to move with her, while maintaining his posture. "That's it. Again. I know you're lifting weights in the gym at our building. You need to find something to exercise your lower extremities."

Urges that had lain dormant inside of Gray for nearly two years woke at the unintentionally suggestive words. First, she was an assault on his senses, and now his brain was filled with naughty ideas about the kind of exercise he'd like to do with her. Make that *used* to do. Make that… Gray stumbled. But Allie was there, holding him until he recovered his balance. Hell, how was he supposed to make love to a woman anymore? Although he'd discussed it with his counseling therapist, they didn't exactly cover the nuts and bolts of that in physical therapy.

"Maybe you should walk more at work," she suggested, "and not spend so much time in your wheelchair, hovering over your microscope and equipment in the lab."

"Crimes aren't going to solve themselves. I have to work. People can't wait for me to get from my lab to a meeting. The lab is a big building. There's a lot of ground to cover." Now he was just getting frustrated with himself for being less than the man he used to be—literally. Every time he thought he'd learned to accept his fate and settle into his new normal, a cruel voice laughed inside his head. *So, you think you're attracted to this woman? Ha. What are you going to do about it?*

Nothing.

He'd be her neighbor. He'd be her patient. He'd be her friend.

But he wasn't going to jeopardize any of that or embarrass himself by trying to be something more.

But Allie's teasing reprimands and positivity weren't going to stop. "Maybe you could leave the lab and go work actual crimes scenes."

"I've worked crime scenes. When my chair or the possibility of dropping my crutches won't jeopardize the integrity of the evidence." That didn't give him as many opportunities to get out into the field as he liked, but he wouldn't jeopardize his work or that of any of the other criminalists he worked with by adding his own tracks or trace to a scene. "Besides, the bulk of blood analysis is done in the lab. I can evaluate blood spatter or spray patterns from the pictures other members of my team bring me."

"Okay." They reached the end of the walkway, with Allie still holding him like a dance partner and encouraging him to move with her. "Then take up running," she suggested.

He snorted at that, scarcely aware that he'd turned without having to grab the railings or lean on her.

Then they were *dancing*, step-by-step, back down the walkway. "Seriously. Look into a pair of prostheses with curved blades. Like that runner from South Africa. Who supposedly murdered his girlfriend. And I'm guessing someone like you from their crime lab helped put him away."

She stopped moving and her voice trailed off. Her hand slipped from his shoulder down to the crook of his elbow, and he could see her thoughts turning inward to a sad or troubling memory. Had the mention of a dangerous boyfriend triggered something she'd rather forget?

"Allie?" Gray squeezed the hand he still held.

She shook off those troubling thoughts and moved her free hand back to his shoulder, giving him a nudge to straighten him back into place. He hadn't even realized he'd leaned toward her. He did realize it took several seconds for her gray-blue gaze to tilt up to his again. But she was smiling. Maybe she was simply empathetic to what had been a tragic news story. "I run several times a week. It's a great stress reducer for me. That's the time I'm supposed to think through my to-do list and solve all the world's problems, but I find it's usually thirty to forty minutes of not thinking about anything at all. Mentally, I find it very relaxing. Plus, it keeps my lungs and leg muscles strong, and allows me to indulge in the ice cream I love without putting any more weight on my hips and butt. You might find it helpful, too. It gives you those exercise endorphins you must crave, and keeps you from being a grump. But you won't get top-heavy."

Gray's gaze dropped to said hips and butt, not seeing anything he didn't like about those curves. Then he realized he was eyeballing her, and that she'd danced him back to the opposite end of the walkway before he saw another man's hand reaching toward her. He instinctively slipped his hand to the small of her back and tightened his grip, pulling her hips into his. But the impulse to turn and put himself between Allie and the perceived threat didn't come fast enough.

"You flirtin' with my patient, Tate?" Another physical therapist, dressed in nylon running pants and a polo, settled his fingers atop Allie's shoulder.

Doug Friesen seemed oblivious to the way Allie flinched away from his touch and ducked beneath the railing to the opposite side of the walkway, releasing Gray, as well. "I was keeping an eye on Gray while you were helping Ben. Mrs. Burroughs still has a few minutes left on the stationary bike. Maeve is watching her now. Her patient was a no-show." She glanced over to the striking older woman with gray streaks in her dark hair, sighing at the woman's responding wink and thumbs-up, which seemed to imply there was something romantic about her impromptu *dance* with Gray. Allie shook her head at the shameless matchmaking before patting Gray's arm. "I know this guy is a perfectionist. I could see his posture flagging, and I knew that exercising in that position wasn't going to help those back spasms he's been having."

Doug studied Gray's alignment and frowned. "Are you saying I'm not doing my job right?"

Allie shrugged at his mildly defensive tone. "I'm saying we're a team here, and since we're understaffed and usually have to cover more than one patient, we help each other out where needed." She nodded toward the medically retired Army sergeant at the dexterity table who was adjusting to his new life with one hand. "Your session with Ben was running long. Maeve is keeping Mrs. Burroughs from trying to set me up with her son and every man in the room between twenty and eighty. In return, I keep your patient moving when you're otherwise occupied. Plus, I'm covering for Maeve a couple of hours on Saturday morning."

"Of course. Thanks." Doug thumbed over his shoulder to the table where he'd set up a new puzzle block challenge for Ben Hunter to practice with the prosthetic hook on his left arm. "You sure you don't want to trade with me? Sergeant Hunter is in a snit about something. Said he'd rather work with you than anybody else. It took longer than I expected to convince him to stay for therapy today and work with me. Sorry about that, Captain." Even though he'd asked him to use his given name, Doug had once told Gray that his service in the Army National Guard had ingrained in him the habit of calling the veterans he worked with by their rank. "Let me see you make the walk one more time, and then I'll get you on the massage table for a few minutes to put some heat packs on you."

Ignoring the knots in his hips and back, Gray dutifully retraced his steps. But his gaze was focused on Allie. Her butt formed a perfect heart shape as she bent over to pick up a towel that had fallen to the floor. That woman did not need to worry about her love for ice cream. Those curves were somehow both athletic and lush. Between their hips and chests brushing against each other, her willingness to touch him and that particularly lovely view, his manhood had perked up with a distinct interest in the friendly blonde who lived in the apartment next to his. But he was certain that having sex with his funny, smart, delectable neighbor wasn't the sort of lower body exercise the PT had in mind.

Gray and Allie were friends. Neighbors. He hitched a ride with her to physical therapy on the mornings he had a session before work, or carpooled home when he came in afterward, like today. Sometimes they ran errands together since he was still getting comfortable driving the van with hand controls he'd been trained on. He'd opened a pickle jar for her and disposed of the mouse trap she'd set for the little friend who'd invaded the cabinet under her kitchen sink this past winter. They'd bonded over the fact they were both veterans, and they both loved thin-crust pizza and Kansas City Chiefs football.

Even before today's overt awareness of all things

Allie Tate had caught him off guard, he'd considered asking her out on a date. But what was the point? He'd occasionally seen a man *walk* up to her door to take her out. He couldn't do that. He enjoyed her company, admired her self-sufficiency and appreciated her humor so much that he felt like a creeper for fantasizing about taking their friend-zone relationship to the next level, like any normal man would. But Grayson Malone, who'd left his legs and two of his best friends back in the Middle East, wasn't a normal man. He needed metal rods and suction cups, or that damned wheelchair, to get around. Hell, he wasn't even sure how he would make love to a woman anymore. The plumbing still worked, judging by his body's stirring interest in Allie, but rods of cold titanium and a patchwork of scars around both stumps were hardly a turn-on. What if she physically recoiled like Brittany had? Or even politely glanced away? How was he supposed to brace himself without hurting her? Or even put himself inside her when he needed both hands to stay upright? Not to mention how studly his appeal must be after plopping down on his butt or landing on his face because he'd tripped over his nonexistent feet.

"Gray? Malone!" Allie's touch on his arm interrupted his deep thoughts.

"Huh?"

"You were a million miles away."

Actually, his thoughts had been right here in this room. On the woman standing beside him, her eyes narrowed as if his preoccupation worried her. "I'm sorry. It's been a long day. What did you ask me?"

"Do you need a ride home this evening? I'm not sure how you got here from work. I didn't see your van out front. I was going to order some takeout and pick it up on the way home. Otherwise, I'm heading straight there."

"Jackson dropped me off."

Allie's eyes widened, maybe trying to place his friend from the crime lab. "The big guy?"

Gray nodded.

"He's hasn't been waiting for you this whole time, has he?"

Jackson Dobbs? Sitting in a room surrounded by this many people he didn't know? Not likely. "I sent him home. I've got a car scheduled to pick me up."

"You didn't drive your van?" she asked.

Man, he had been lost inside his head. When had Doug circled around behind Allie? True, the brown-haired guy was retrieving Gray's metal crutches, but generally, Gray was hyperaware of his surroundings. Observing the people around him had been too deeply ingrained in him by the Corps.

"I'm not a hundred percent confident with my reflexes," he answered honestly, meeting Allie's gaze. "So, I try to avoid rush hour traffic. Especially after dark."

"Then let me drive you," she offered. "Save the money. We're going to the same place."

He shook his head. "It's enough of an imposition

getting me here to PT. You don't need to be hauling me around the city."

"It's *not* an imposition. If I've ever made you feel like that, I'm sorry."

There was a difference between not being an imposition, and actually being needed. Wanted for something more than opening pickle jars and disposing of dead rodents.

Gray accepted the crutches Doug handed him and slipped them on to his forearms. The tension around Allie's mouth hadn't been there a few seconds ago. It made him want to lighten her mood. "Not to worry. I've got PT again on Friday morning. I could use a ride then."

Her smile felt like a hell of a reward for a simple carpool invitation. "How about you drive on Friday," she suggested. "It'll give you more practice with the hand controls. And since the days are starting to get longer, you won't be driving at night on the way home. I get off work early on Friday, so you could pick me up, and we'd get there before sunset."

The tension returned as Doug touched the small of her back. "I thought you and I could catch dinner and a movie on Friday night. You said you'd like to do that sometime."

"I'm sorry, Doug." She turned and retreated a step from her coworker, a step closer to Gray. "Thanks for asking. But I'm working Saturday morning, so I don't want to be out late."

"I'll give you a ride home Friday if you need it," the other man offered.

"It's more convenient if Gray does it. We live in the same building, down the hall from each other. You live across the city. It would be hugely out of your way."

Even with his rusty people skills, it was easy to pick up on Allie's discomfort with Doug and her attempt to let him down without hurting his feelings. Gray leaned his hands into the grips of his crutches and stepped up beside her. "If you trust me to drive you, I'd be happy to chauffeur you around. I could use the practice."

Her delicate nostrils flared with a sigh of relief. "I don't mind riding in your van if you don't mind squeezing into my Accord. Gas prices are nuts right now, anyway. Let's carpool and save money. I'll drive tonight—you take Friday."

"You having money issues?" Doug asked. Even Gray cringed at the tactless question. "All the more reason for me to give you a ride."

"You'll do no such thing." She smiled as she said the words, but Gray wasn't imagining the way her hands fisted in the towel. "I'm trying to save the planet. Help Gray with his occupational therapy. And—" she glanced up at Gray again "—have someone to talk to during the boring commute. You know, like friends do?"

"I can talk to you friendly-like," Doug insisted.

Gray read the silent plea in her eyes. There was

something else besides a neighborly favor between friends going on here. But whether Allie was trying to avoid Doug, specifically, or something else, he couldn't tell. He wouldn't avoid those instincts that told him something was off with his next-door neighbor. The last time he'd ignored that little warning voice that said something wasn't right, he'd come home to Kansas City a double amputee.

He might not be a fully functional warrior anymore, but he could be a friend and help Allie out. Even if all she needed from him was an excuse to avoid Doug.

"All right. I'll cancel my car tonight. We're getting takeout for two, though—and I'm paying for it. Also, I'd appreciate the backup when I drive on Friday—just in case my coordination is off, or I get distracted making sure I'm doing everything right."

Allie's smile of relief bloomed across her face. "I'd love to ride shotgun with you."

Doug's noisy grunt made him sound like he was about thirteen years old. "Looks like Sergeant Hunter is about to have a meltdown. I'll get him started on the treadmill—let him run off that temper." He eyed the young woman with the short brunette hair chatting with Mrs. Burroughs before nodding to Gray. "I'll see if Maeve is free on Friday. Don't leave before I get those heat packs on your back and do today's exit survey."

"I won't."

Once Doug was out of earshot, Allie groaned beside Gray. "Why do I feel like I've just thrown Maeve under the bus?"

"I'm happy to help out with whatever that was. But will my wheelchair fit in your car? I'll still give you the out and stick with my car service."

"We'll make it fit. Possibly in the back seat if it won't go in the trunk." Allie smiled up at Gray. "I appreciate the help more than you know." She glanced back at Doug before squeezing Gray's arm and excusing herself. "I need to rescue Maeve and get Mrs. Burroughs through her electric-pulse treatment on her hip. See you in about twenty-five minutes. I owe you one, Gray." She tilted her gray-blue eyes up to his. "You're my hero."

Chapter Two

Allie carried Grayson's crutches onto the elevator and held the doors open while he rolled his wheelchair inside. The entire ride home she wondered how the friendly—and dare she say flirty?—vibe they'd shared at the PT clinic had become dark and closed off. The many moods of Grayson Malone were as confusing as they were intriguing. What had she said or done to send him so deep inside his head that the only words he'd spoken on the drive home had been to give his order to the Chinese restaurant where they'd stopped to pick up dinner?

As much as his unexplained silences ticked her off—after all, she was a medical professional and a veteran, to boot, who had some experience helping vets deal with reintegrating into civilian life and post-traumatic stress—something twisted in her heart to imagine the pain or frustration or flashback or regret he was dealing with all by himself right now.

Although she would have happily walked beside him at his pace from her car through the parking garage, he'd insisted on removing his prostheses and using his wheelchair. He'd said his back was hurting after the physical therapy session, which probably wasn't a lie. But she suspected he was self-conscious about his awkward gait and moving slowly with his prosthetic limbs as much as any kind of physical pain he might be feeling. Her tall, broad-shouldered neighbor with the intelligent green eyes and dark blond hair still cut in its high and tight style from his Marine Corps years wasn't the first disabled veteran she'd worked with at the physical therapy center.

But he was the only one who'd ever sparked any interest. The only one she'd ever seen as something more than a patient. The only one she'd *danced* with.

That thought should have scared her.

But she'd still turned to him for help this evening.

And he'd been in a brooding, distant mood ever since.

"Thanks for the save," she said after they entered the elevator, while she waited for Gray to spin his chair to face the front. Then, she pushed the button for the third floor and tried once more to generate a neutral, neighborly conversation to get them back to where they'd been less than two hours ago. "There are only so many ways I can say no to Doug, and I've tried them all. But he keeps asking me out. Plus, he's the handsy type. He finds ways to touch me at work all the time. It's always impersonal, nothing overtly sexual, but it doesn't stop."

"You don't like Doug?" Gray adjusted the bags of Chinese takeout over the gym bag on his lap.

She tried not to jump at his astute response, then realized this conversation was heading into her own dangerous territory.

"I'm kind of off men and dating right now," she admitted without explaining why. "I moved to Kansas City for a fresh start. I haven't even been here a year yet. I want to stand on my own two feet and settle into this new version of my life now that I've left the Navy behind me."

The Navy wasn't the only thing she'd left behind in Florida.

"You don't want to be tied to anyone right now," Gray clarified.

"Not the way Doug wants. I'm willing to be friends. But my patience is wearing thin. I can't tell if he's clueless or doesn't care that I'm not interested the way he is. Maybe he thinks persistence will change my mind." Allie shrugged. "I don't even think he's that into me. It's the thrill of conquest he likes. Hence his eagerness to hit on Maeve seconds after I shot him down."

"You need to flat out tell him no."

Allie shook her head with a wry smile. "I have to work with him. I don't want to make things awkward between us."

"It's already awkward for you." She heard the innate command of an officer in Gray's tone. At least, that clipped authority was better than the perfunctory silences they'd shared on the ride home. "That's not fair. Tell him no."

"Maybe if I told him I had a boyfriend, he'd back off." She sighed at how high school that solution sounded. "But then I'd have to come up with someone to play the part."

Allie eyed the prime candidate across from her. For one wild second, she considered asking for his help with that, too. The idea of Grayson Malone claiming her as his woman wasn't repugnant. Even with his mood swings from sexy protector to mysterious grump, it wasn't repugnant at all. But *she* was the one who didn't want to be in a relationship—real or fake—right now. The last one had nearly killed her.

Oh, God. She hoped she wasn't attracted to Gray because some subconscious part of her brain thought his wheelchair or prosthetic legs made him seem weaker than Noah Boggs had been—like she could take him in a physical fight if she had to. Allie shook her head, dismissing the thought as soon as the possibility had flitted through her brain. Standing upright, Grayson Malone was a man who made her feel petite, sheltered, feminine. And that upper body strength was no joke. Even with part of it missing, his body was in better shape than Noah's had been. Allie's skin prickled with goose bumps at the thought of sitting in Gray's lap, snugging herself against his hard chest and feeling those arms wrap around her. And though there was a bleakness to those dark green eyes right now, she'd seen kindness there. Alertness.

Humor and intelligence, too. Noah's eyes had been cold and smug, and at the end, full of rage.

No, she wasn't attracted to Gray because he was weak or controllable. She was attracted to him because he was interesting and intelligent and handsome. She was attracted to his strength—be it physical, character or intellectual—and the certainty that he'd never use that strength against her.

She curled her fingers into her palm, resisting the urge to stroke them across Gray's lightly stubbled jaw. The elevator filled with the delicious scents of cashew chicken and crab Rangoon, along with the more subtle scent of Gray—slightly musky from working out, slightly spicy from his soap or shampoo, and completely masculine in a way that woke feminine impulses in her that she didn't want to acknowledge.

Besides, she had a feeling his answer to faking a relationship would be no, if not *hell no*, judging by the way Gray stared straight ahead at the steel doors.

Deflecting any concern he might have for her relationship with her coworker, Allie broke the awkward silence and switched topics. "Carpooling on the days we're going to the same location at the same time makes economic and environmental sense. And I'm serious about you practicing your driving. You've had that van for four months now. I know the snow and ice we had this past winter made it tricky to learn. Theoretically, though, you could drive a regular car as long as you have your prosthetic legs on. It's time for you to own how far you've come in your recovery."

The doors opened onto the third floor, and he gestured for her to precede him out. "I worry that I'm more of a menace to other people than myself."

"Why do you do that?" Getting a little fed up with this particularly negative mood, she turned on him the moment he rolled up beside her. "You always deflect compliments and words of encouragement. Why do you make light of the fact you survived a war zone? Transitioned into a cool new civilian job? Come through countless surgeries and psychological therapy? Mastered your chair *and* walking *and* driving again? I know you're still dealing with post-traumatic stress, mourning the guys in your unit you lost and getting used to your new normal. But you've conquered more in two years than most men tackle in a lifetime. I'm in awe of you, Gray. I see your success, not your shortcomings."

His eyes locked on to hers for several charged moments before he dismissed her vehement speech and rolled past her toward their apartments. "Therapy session is over, Allie. I'm your neighbor, not your patient, certainly not your *hero*. Let's eat dinner and call it a night."

Was that what this mood swing was all about? Because she'd been grateful enough to thank him for stepping up when she'd needed a friend? She rolled her eyes before following. Stubborn man. For a few minutes at the clinic when he'd put his hand on her waist and they'd practically danced, and then when he'd pulled her body flush with his to avoid Doug's touch, she thought they'd made a connection beyond being neighbors. Certainly, the interest she'd felt stirring behind his zipper meant he wasn't completely immune to her. She'd even imagined what it would be like if they were really dancing. At five-nine, she was on the tall side for a woman, and was still as fit and athletic as she'd been on active duty, maybe even more so after her dealings with Noah. But Gray stood half a foot taller, making her feel feminine and almost delicate when she stood close to him. He was the perfect height for her to lean in and tuck her forehead against the juncture of his neck and shoulder. And then he'd answered her silent plea for help. Like a real hero, he'd had her back when she'd needed someone. Allie swore she'd felt something a little like lust and a lot more than affection stirring deep inside her.

She'd needed an excuse *not* to accept any favors from Doug Friesen. He already made working at the clinic uncomfortable with his innuendos about wanting to be more than coworkers. But she didn't want to tell him to go suck an egg, or to break his wrist if he touched her one more time, because she'd still have to come back and work an eight-hour shift with him the next day.

Allie had already had her fill of men who wouldn't take no for an answer.

Even more than a practical desire to avoid any awkwardness at work, especially around the patients—Doug didn't spark any frissons of lust or affection in her. She supposed he was good-looking in a preppy, class president sort of way. He was a skilled therapist, had a good rapport with his patients. But he didn't draw her eye when he walked across the room. He didn't challenge her with his wit and intelligence. He didn't make her tingle.

She had male friends, from both her time in the Navy and here in Kansas City. Since moving to the Midwest, she'd forced herself to go on a few dates—some good, some bad—but none were memorable. She'd gone into the Navy to get her medical training and see something of the world. In some ways, she'd seen far too much, and had been ready to move closer to her folks, who lived in a small town in central Missouri, when her commitment was up. She had a solid, rewarding career. But she wasn't going to settle for a guy like Doug. Nice, maybe, but blah. Boring. Inconsiderate. She wanted more.

Allie desperately wanted to tingle.

Inhaling a deep breath, she watched Gray unlock the door to the apartment next to hers. Damn. Look who made her tingle. A moody, wounded Marine whose protective alpha nature snuck out when he wasn't thinking about his legs and scars.

More than that tingle of awareness, Allie wanted to feel safe.

She wasn't sure any man could pull off that miracle anymore. Doug didn't make her feel safe. Her ex-boyfriend certainly hadn't. Even restraining orders from both the Navy and a civil judge against Noah Boggs didn't make her feel completely safe.

She couldn't say that Grayson Malone made her feel safe. After all, he was a patient of hers, theoretically making her the stronger member of their relationship. Yes, he was a decorated Marine, but he used his brain more than his fractured body now. She wasn't certain he could stop the threat she felt lurking in the corners of her life.

But she trusted him.

Grayson was a good man. He was a criminalist at the crime lab, specializing in blood analysis and chemistry. And yeah, with those muscular shoulders, close-cropped hair and piercing green eyes, she could see traces of the Marine he once had been. His self-confidence might have taken a serious hit, since he'd clearly been a physical man before his injuries. But he was funny and considerate—when his demons and self-doubts didn't shut him down. And he'd caught on to her plea to not leave her alone with Doug on Friday night.

She'd embrace that trust. Let her guard down for the hour or so they'd share over dinner and be grateful that there was at least one man in this world she didn't have to worry about hurting her.

Allie reached her own door and inserted the key before speaking again. "I'm going to change out of my work clothes and wash my face. I'll be over in about ten minutes to eat." Or, since he'd done her a favor with Doug, maybe she'd do him the favor of letting him brood all by his moody self. "If you still want the company. Otherwise, I can take my food now and say good night."

"No." With deft precision, he spun his chair in the open doorway and faced her. "Sorry I turned into such a downer. Sometimes, I wish my emotions were as easy to process as a piece of evidence is." Those green eyes drilled into hers. "But I'd like the company. If you can put up with me."

Eloquence aside, as apologies went, that one was pretty sweet. "I've put up with worse than you, Malone," she teased.

"In your line of work, Tate, I bet you have." The harsh line of Gray's mouth softened with the hint of a smile, and he rolled his chair into his apartment. "I'll stick the food in the microwave to keep it warm. See you in ten."

Relieved that they seemed to be on friendly footing again, Allie opened her door...and froze in her tracks. Her jaw gaped open at the utter devastation that greeted her.

Payback.

The single word was written in crimson paint—at least she hoped it was paint—over and over, across her TV screen, the front of her grandmother's hutch, the bank of cabinets hanging above her kitchen peninsula, and in varying sizes and designs across every wall.

So much rage. So much destruction. The blood seemed to drain from her head to her toes, leaving her shivering in its wake.

Blips of memory—fear that she was losing her mind, harsh words, hard fists, cruel humiliation—flashed through her brain. Not again. She'd done her part. She thought she'd left her nightmare behind. But this twisted…sick…rage…

Allie swallowed hard and searched for her voice.

"Gray?" The word came out on a strangled gasp. She pushed back her fear and retreated from the gruesome sight. She was a fighter. That was why she was here now. That was why she was alive at all. Because she fought back. "Gray?" Air finally poured into her lungs, and she screamed. "Gray!"

Allie stumbled down the hallway. Gray was already out his door, pumping his wheelchair toward her. "Allie? What's wrong?"

She met him halfway, digging her fingers into the shoulder of his fleece hoodie. He wrapped a hand around her forearm, his narrowed eyes demanding an explanation. "Someone's been in my apartment. It's…awful."

"Is the intruder still there?" He pulled his cell phone from his pocket and pushed forward.

"I don't think so. But I didn't get past the entryway. And I didn't stick around to look."

"Get inside my apartment. Lock the door behind you."

Instead of obeying his orders, Allie fell into step behind him, still clinging to his shoulder. "You can't go in there by yourself. If he's still there, you'll need backup."

Besides, she didn't want to be alone, not when she was on the verge of forgetting every bit of training she'd had and panicking.

"You think I need backup?" he asked, hesitating.

"This doesn't have a damn thing to do with your legs." She flipped open the can of pepper spray she carried. "Every soldier needs backup."

Every sailor did, too.

He nodded sharply, his green eyes meeting hers. "All right. But you stay behind me. And don't accidentally shoot me with that stuff."

Allie scanned up and down the empty hallway. "I won't."

Gray nudged open her door and cursed, looking at the blood. Something that looked like blood. It was still awful. Still unsettling. Still so full of hate.

"Eyes on me, Lieutenant," Gray ordered. Startled by his command, she automatically obeyed. He rested his hand over hers, forcing Allie to retreat from the horrific sight as he rolled away from the opening. He punched in 911. She kept her gaze locked on his as the dispatcher picked up. He quickly identified himself as an adjunct of KCPD, gave their address and asked for the police. He squeezed her trembling hand in his. “I’m going to need a team from the crime lab here, too.”

Chapter Three

"It's blood." Gray watched the end of the swab turn pink, confirming his suspicion. He dropped the phenolphthalein reagent into his kit beside his chair, then secured the swab with the trace he'd swiped off Allie's living room wall in a sterile evidence tube before labeling it and stowing it in his evidence kit, as well. He looked over to his team leader, Lexi Callahan-Murphy, who was numbering and photographing the impressions in the carpet and on a sofa cushion that could indicate the size of shoe, if not an actual shoe print, worn by the intruder. "Every sample from every surface I've retrieved—it's all presumptive positive for blood."

Lexi tucked a strand of the light brown hair that hung from beneath her CSI ball cap behind her ear and looked up from her work. "Human blood?"

"I'd have to type it at the lab to confirm. There may be some animal blood mixed in. Just from the sheer volume—the perp would have to have cleaned out a blood bank to get this much. But again, I want to run these samples in the lab before making any definitive conclusion."

Zoe Stockman, the rookie on the crime lab's C team, plucked a fiber from the carpet near the baseboard with her tweezers and studied it in the beam of her flashlight. "This is too thick and coarse to be a human hair. It looks like it has blood on it, though." She clenched the flashlight between her teeth to secure the fiber in an evidence envelope. "Could have come from a paintbrush," she suggested.

Although she still hadn't developed the confidence the rest of the team shared while processing a scene, especially after a disastrous experience with the former criminalist who'd been her mentor, Gray believed in Zoe's technical proficiency. "I suspect you're right," he agreed. "Looks like a lot of this was painted on. Some of it was thrown, obviously," he said, nodding toward the spatter of red droplets on the couch and wall. "Whoever it was had to have had plenty of uninterrupted time to make this big a mess."

Ever the team builder, and attuned to the needs of the criminalists she supervised, Lexi smiled at Zoe. "Good work, Zo. One fiber isn't a lot to go on, but you might be able to trace the make and manufacturer, and then give us an idea on where our perp might have purchased it."

A faint smile replaced the flashlight on Zoe's lips. "I'll make it my priority back at the lab tomorrow."

Her gaze darted briefly to his. “You know, since Gray’s a friend and all.”

He offered her a curt nod. “Appreciate it.”

Gray rolled his chair back a couple of feet to take in the damage and violation of what should have been Allie’s safe haven from the world. He wasn’t a detective, but he’d learned to read the enemy well enough in his time with the Marines in the Middle East and other hot spots around the world. Whoever had done this was very angry and extremely obsessed with Allie.

Payback was a personal message.

But what could his pretty, practical, strong-willed neighbor have done to anyone that would warrant this kind of threat?

It was late, and hunger gnawed at the walls of his stomach from the dinner he’d missed. But Gray’s analytical brain was running on all cylinders, cataloging the movement of criminalists and police officers around Allie’s once-tidy apartment, as well as thinking back to his worst day in the Corps and a more recent trial where his expert testimony had helped put away a disturbed young man who’d murdered three women. When the rocket-propelled grenade had hit his convoy carrying weapons and explosives from the base to the front line, there’d been plenty of blood to go around—the scattered body parts of his dead and wounded buddies, the shredded muscles and arteries hanging from his own shattered bones. In court, he’d explained how the young man had drained the blood from his victims, much like a coroner preparing a body for a funeral. It was his analysis of the jars of blood stored in the suspect's basement, and the trace amounts of embalming chemicals he'd found in them, that had linked Jamie Kleinschmidt to the three women and secured his conviction. He suspected there had been even more victims, but three confirmed kills were enough to secure a place for Kleinschmidt on Missouri's death row.

Allie's apartment wasn't a murder scene or a war zone. But there was a hell of a lot of blood here, too.

And a hell of a lot of questions he needed answers to.

Gray rubbed at the sweats covering his muscular thighs, willing the phantom pain that sparked through the nerves at the end of his stumps to recede. The fact that he was feeling anything there at all had become a signal that something was off. About the crime scene? About Allie? With himself? Something was nagging in the recesses of his brain that he needed to check before he lost the effectiveness and objectivity necessary to complete his mission—er, to do his job.

Usually, Grayson possessed a clinical mind that allowed him to separate his science from his emotions. He'd survived on that battlefield by being able to separate his pain and fear and grief from the medical training necessary to keep himself from bleeding out and dying until another team could get to him. But the threats painted on Allie's walls and furniture bothered him more than the sounds and smells of battlefield triage or the gruesome collection of trophies he'd cataloged in a serial killer's basement. He was a wounded Marine who'd seen and dealt out death. A chemist and criminalist who analyzed the aftermath of a victim's worst day.

This should be just another crime scene he needed to process.

Only, as he watched Allie hugging her arms beneath her breasts, her hips rocking against the edge of the countertop in her kitchen like the nervous tapping of a foot while she dutifully answered questions from the dark-haired female officer assigned to the case, Gray knew this was anything but another crime scene.

The urge to protect Allie tightened the muscles across his arms and chest, while his hands fisted around the wheels of his chair. Grayson wanted to go to her. He wanted to be her champion the way he had been earlier that evening at the clinic when Doug Friesen wouldn't keep his hands off her. In the elevator she'd even hinted that he could pretend to be her boyfriend to help keep Friesen's unwanted attention at bay. But Gray didn't want to do *pretend* with a woman. He didn't know whether to feel flattered that she saw him as a worthy candidate to be her partner or insulted that she believed *fake* was the only kind of relationship he could handle. Hell, he shouldn't even be considering a relationship—real or pretend.

Allie was a veteran Navy lieutenant, strong both physically and mentally. She didn't need a man to take over, but she could use a friend to stand beside her, a fellow veteran to have her back while she dealt with the job in front of her. Gray could see that today had taken a toll on her, and his moodiness hadn't helped. Despite the healthy natural glow of her skin, he could see the shadows beneath her eyes, and read the tension bracketing her mouth as she discussed the break-in with Officer Cutler.

The reality was Grayson Malone wasn't anybody's champion. Not anymore. He forced his grip to relax. He couldn't take his chair through her apartment, as the wheel tracks might compromise the foot impressions and blood spatter in the carpet. If he avoided the taped-off path they suspected the intruder had taken from one bloody message to the next, he'd have to move furniture to maneuver his chair. And with the other members of his CSI team, Officer Cutler and Allie herself watching, Gray wasn't about to crawl to the kitchen on his arms and stumps the way he often navigated his own apartment.

His newly fitted prosthetic limbs were in their bag, down the hall, inside his apartment. By the time he'd considered retrieving them and putting them on so he could move around more like a normal man, the moment that Allie needed support and comfort had passed. Now she was striding out of the kitchen ahead of Officer Cutler, heading toward the open door where Lexi's husband, Officer Aiden Murphy, and his K-9 partner, Blue, were patrolling the hallway to keep the scene clear of curious neighbors.

Like his, the apartment was small enough that there were no private conversations unless someone whispered. "I've been gone since early this morning," Allie explained to the shorter woman. "Went for a run and then drove to work. I showered and changed into my scrubs there."

Officer Cutler did the math. "That gave our perp about thirteen hours without interruption to do this." She jotted the information in her notes. "I'll check with the neighbors and building staff to see if anyone heard any activity during that time frame." She glanced past Allie to Shane Duvall. The bearded and bespectacled single dad was dusting the door locks and frame for prints. "Any signs of forced entry?"

"None." Shane snapped a picture of a print he'd found on the doorknob before lifting the print with tape and sealing it. "The intruder had access. I don't even see pick marks in the lock."

Jackson Dobbs, a big, quiet man, and probably Gray's best friend at the lab, was working beside Shane. "We'll need your prints, ma'am."

Gray rolled a few inches closer. "You'll need to exclude mine, too. I opened the door after Allie noticed the break-in."

Jackson simply nodded.

"Could you have forgotten to lock your door this morning?" Officer Cutler asked.

Allie's ponytail whipped back and forth against

her shoulders as she shook her head. "I don't forget that. Ever."

Gina Cutler paused a moment at Allie's vehement denial before making a note. "So, we're looking for someone who has a key. Or who had the opportunity to make a copy of yours."

"I haven't given a spare key to anyone." Allie's gaze darted to Gray's. "Not even a neighbor if I should get locked out. I keep my keys in my bag at work in a locker with a combination lock. Otherwise, they're on me."

"*Is* there a spare key?" Gina asked. "Where do you keep it?"

"It's taped inside my mailbox downstairs."

"Shane." Lexi ordered her teammate to process the second key.

Shane closed his kit and headed out the door. "I'm on it." He held out his hand for Allie's mailbox key. "I'll dust the key and mailbox for prints. And I'll see if the tape has been replaced recently or has any trace on it. I should also be able to tell if a copy was made."

Allie removed the mailbox key from her key ring but seemed reluctant to hand it over. Had Gray ever realized how paranoid she was about restricting access to her apartment? Seeing her hesitation, he brushed his plastic-gloved fingertips across her forearm, hating that she startled at even that light touch. "You can trust Shane, Allie. I'll vouch for him."

Her lips curved into a brief smile, and she handed over the key. "Of course. You're just doing your job."

"Yes, ma'am," Shane assured her. He clasped the key in his hand. "I'll bring this back, I promise. And I'll let you know if I see any signs of tampering with your mailbox."

"Thank you." She exchanged a nod with Shane, and he headed to the stairs at the end of the hallway.

"The building super has a master key," Gray pointed out, inching his chair closer to Allie's side before turning to face Officer Cutler. "You should check out who has access to that set of keys, as well."

Gina made that note, too. "Just a couple more questions, Ms. Tate. Does it look like anything's missing?"

Allie heaved an impatient sigh. "You asked me that already."

"And now that you've had a little time to think about it, I'm asking you again." Gina made no apology for doing her job well. "Oftentimes, after the initial shock of something like this wears off, the person I'm interviewing can remember more details."

After holding the other woman's gaze for a moment, Allie dutifully surveyed her apartment again. While the main rooms of her apartment had been vandalized, nothing of conventional value, like the big-screen TV, the laptop on her kitchen table or what looked like some genuine antiques inside her hutch, had been taken.

"Nothing that I've noticed." Allie pulled her hands inside the sleeves of the fitted running shirt she wore under her scrub top, tugging the ends down past her fingertips and poking her thumbs through the wrist holes.

Was she cold? Was the fear and feeling of violation getting to her? Were those subtle, almost constant movements of her fingers and arms and swaying posture her way of dispelling nervous energy so that she could hold on to her patience and rational thought? Or were they signs of a crack in her protective armor?

Instinctively needing to support her in some way, to let the fellow veteran know that he had her back when she needed him, Gray unzipped the gray hoodie he wore and shrugged out of it.

"Can you tell if anything new has been added?" Gina asked.

Allie frowned at the question. "New? Like what?"

"A hidden camera? A love letter? A more specific threat?" Gina Cutler was a pint-size dynamo who'd been a top candidate for KCPD's SWAT teams until getting shot on a routine patrol call took her out of the running. But she'd honed her empathetic instincts and street smarts to become one of the department's most skilled investigators. "Most of the cases I handle now are women and minors who've been victimized. We obviously don't have the whole story yet, but this doesn't feel like a robbery to me. Or random vandalism. It feels very personal."

The color drained from Allie's cheeks as she fisted the end of each sleeve in her fingers and hugged herself. "There's a camera on my laptop, but it's turned off right now. How would I know if I have a hidden camera?"

Jackson Dobbs, ever a man of few words, volunteered. "I'll look." He pushed to his feet and crossed to the back of her apartment to begin his search.

"No notes. No threats—beyond the obvious." Allie shrugged. "No spare body parts in my freezer or knife stuck in my great-grandmother's doll or men's boxer shorts in my lingerie drawer." Was that her idea of dark humor? Or was she speaking from some kind of experience? Gray couldn't read past the brittle shell of sarcasm surrounding her. But he could see her fingers shaking as she tucked them into her body for warmth or self-comfort.

"Here." Gray handed her his hoodie to put on. When she hesitated to take it, he pushed himself up onto his thighs to drape it around her shoulders. "You're shivering."

"Thanks." For a brief, charged moment, she looked him straight in the eye, as if she was surprised to see him at her level. Then Gray sank back onto his seat, and she shoved her arms into the sleeves of his jacket and zipped it up. "It's probably my adrenaline wearing off rather than being cold."

More than he had for the past several months, Gray wished he was standing on his own two legs so that he could wrap Allie up in his arms and take her away from this scene that so obviously upset her. But what he couldn't do physically, he could still do verbally—take control of the room. "Gina, you done asking her questions?"

"For now."

Gray touched Allie's elbow and nodded toward the doorway. "You should head next door and hang out there while we finish processing—"

"Whoa. Who's cleaning this mess up?" A short, stocky man in tan coveralls appeared in the doorway.

Allie spun around at the interruption, tripping on the wheel of Gray's chair. She would have landed in his lap if his hand on her back and at her waist didn't catch her to keep her upright. Gray tried not to make anything of the fact Allie made no effort to move away from him. Perhaps she wasn't aware of how his hands lingered against her, or how her leg still butted against the end of his thigh. "What are you doing here?"

Before the man who'd startled her could step inside, a warning growl from Aiden Murphy's Belgian Malinois *encouraged* him to raise his hands and back away.

"Easy, Blue." Aiden Murphy warned his K-9 partner to sit. "I need you back in the hallway, sir. This is an active crime scene."

The building superintendent Gray had just mentioned kept his hands in the air, but only retreated beyond the curious poke of Blue's nose. "I work here. This is my building," the thirtysomething man with short, thinning hair explained. "Allie and I are friends." He peeked around the doorframe. "You all right, Al?"

Allie summoned a weak smile. "Yeah, Bubba. I'm okay. I wasn't here when the break-in happened."

Gina clicked her pen to add information to her notepad. "You are…?"

Allie made the introductions. "Officer Cutler, this is our building super, Bubba Summerfield."

"Bubba?" Gina arched a skeptical eyebrow.

"My real name's Jim—James. No one's called me that since I was a kid." Once he realized Blue wasn't going to take a bite out of him, he finally dropped his arms to gesture with them. "This is a good neighborhood. Stuff like this doesn't happen here. This building is filled with veterans and their families. Everybody here are good people. Unless one of them is messed up in the head. Or lost his temper or something. Some of our guys who've been in combat have post-traumatic stress."

With that comment, Allie took a step toward Bubba. "You're not talking about Mr. Malone, are you? He would never hurt me."

"I didn't mean nothin' personal by that, sir." Bubba peeked around her to offer Gray a quick apology before smiling at Allie. "I'm just sayin' I wouldn't expect anybody around here to do something like this." Ignoring both uniformed officers and the dog, Bubba reached for Allie. "You don't need to be afraid, okay? I'll keep a better eye on things. I promise."

Before his grubby fingers ever touched her sleeve, Allie cringed away from his touch. “Please don’t.”

Gray wasn’t the only person in the room who could see that Allie was nearing the end of her rope. With a nod to Gray, Gina shuttled Bubba out of the apartment. “Mr. Summerfield, I’d like to ask you a few questions. Have you been on duty all day?”

“Yeah. Well, I worked my regular nine-to-five shift, and then I’ve been on call this evening.” Bubba spun his finger in the air, indicating the apartment behind them. “Seriously, who cleans this up? Am I going to have to repaint…”

By the time Officer Cutler had steered Bubba down the hallway to continue the interview, Allie had pulled her purse off her shoulder and dug through the contents. “Where is my phone?”

But her shaking hands made it difficult to latch on to things and she was getting more and more frustrated. When her sunglasses and a bag of tissues tumbled out onto the floor, she muttered a curse. Gray scooped up the fallen items, then captured her hand in his firm grip when she reached for them. “Hey.” Finally, the tremors he felt in her dissipated and her gray-blue eyes locked on to his. “You’re usually cool as a cucumber. Tonight, you’re rattled. Talk to me.”

“I’m not rattled.” She followed his glance over to the bloody *Payback* painted on her kitchen cabinets. “Okay, I’m a little rattled,” she admitted, dropping her gaze back to his. “I’m tired. Hungry. And rattled.”

"You have a right to be," he agreed. He stroked his thumb over the back of her knuckles, urging her to explain whatever she was hiding from him.

"I just need to make a phone call. It could be important." She pulled away to deposit the items back inside her purse before resuming a less frantic search. "Is it too late to call Charleston?"

"Charleston, Missouri?" Gray frowned at the seemingly random question. "That's clear on the other side of the state. Down in the Boot Heel."

"Charleston, South Carolina," Allie clarified, still searching.

"What's in South Carolina?" he asked, still not understanding the urgency of her actions.

"NAVCONBRIG CHASN."

Ah, hell. Not so random, after all.

Brig. Navy prison. Gray sat straight back in his chair. What did that have to do with Allie?

Lexi closed up her kit and joined them at the doorway, no doubt reading the wary concern in Gray's posture. "NAVCONBRIG what? What's that?"

Gray answered. "The Naval Consolidated Brig. It's part of a joint base with the US Air Force in South Carolina." But his gaze never left Allie. "You were stationed there?"

She shook her head. "I was stationed in Jacksonville, Florida, before my separation from the Navy and coming here to Kansas City."

The brig in Jacksonville would only house prisoners for a year or so. She was talking about a prison where military hard-timers served out their sentences.

"Who's in the brig in South Carolina? Someone who would do this to you? Someone with friends on the outside who would do this to you?" Lexi exchanged a look with her husband, then met Zoe and Jackson's curious stares. They were all waiting expectantly for her answer. But Allie's eyes stayed focused on Gray. This was not the lead any of Gray or his team had expected to find here tonight. But Allie had been out of the military for less than a year. It was definitely a lead he intended to pursue. He turned his head to Lexi. "Call Chelsea." The crime lab's computer guru could find just about any information any of them ever needed. "Have her look up the number."

"There's no need." Allie had finally found her phone. She pulled it out of her purse and held it up as if she was making a confession. "I have the brig number programmed in my cell."

Chapter Four

"Thank you, Sergeant. Yes. I'll do that." Allie disconnected her phone, shoved it into the pocket of her scrub pants and cursed. "I hate this."

If she hadn't inhaled the crisp, almost icy scent of Gray just then, blended with his own subtle musk on the hoodie she still wore, she might have hurled the phone across the room. But the unfamiliar, blatantly masculine scents reminded her that she wasn't in her own apartment. This wasn't her own space, her own things to take her frustration out on.

But not knowing, not being able to plan a course of action, feeling lost and helpless while she waited to be blindsided by something else—something worse than threats on her apartment walls—left Allie crawling inside her skin. She needed to go for a run—the physical exertion and mind-numbing endorphin release would do her good. She needed to be able to check out from the stress that was eating her up alive for a little while.

Only, the clock on Grayson's stove was ticking

past midnight. It was too late for a woman alone to safely dash through the streets of Kansas City. Sneaking down to the treadmill in the building's workout room didn't hold much appeal, either. With the break-in, she clearly wasn't safe in her own space. Besides, she'd promised Gray she'd stay put so she wouldn't get in the way of the work his team from the crime lab needed to do. And, she'd stay safely locked behind his door so he wouldn't worry, and he could focus on the science that might give her the answers that her phone call to South Carolina had not.

Allie picked at the veggies in her Snow-White Chicken, wishing she had something to contribute to Gray's team besides staying out of their way. After he'd settled her into his apartment, pointed out where the necessaries were located, and encouraged her to make herself at home, he'd locked her in and gone back next door. He and his team had to finish processing her apartment and other parts of the building they thought might provide a clue as to who'd broken into her sanctuary and defaced it with the vile, blood-soaked threats.

Her phone call to South Carolina had only ratcheted up the tension inside her to the point that, five hours after discovering the break-in, she ached from stress. She'd gotten the party line in military speak—but no answers. The hour was late. The office staff had gone home for the evening. She needed to contact the staff of the Marine Corps colonel currently serving as the warden during office hours or try to do some research online. Depending on national security issues, the information she wanted might not be public record, anyway. After setting the alarm on her phone to call the brig office back at 9:01 a.m. Eastern time, Allie resigned herself to a sleepless night like the ones she'd known back in Jacksonville.

The layers of command sounding concerned and supportive, all while covering their asses and doing nothing, felt far too familiar. She'd lost so much and fought so hard to do the right thing two years ago. She thought she was stronger now—physically and mentally. But that sense of violation—that powerless feeling of standing alone against the enemy when she'd opened her door and read the bloody threats—had taken her right back to the nightmare she thought time and distance had erased.

With her body running on fumes, but her brain unwilling to shut down, Allie busied herself cleaning up Grayson's kitchen. She was surprised to discover that he was a bit of a slob, with a couple days' worth of dishes stacked in his sink and on the stove. A mystery sauce had hardened on one pan and a plate like glue, but she needed to keep her hands busy. So, she loaded the dishwasher and ran it. She even washed the pan and a steak knife and spatula by hand and left the items on the placemat on his table to dry.

Stay busy. Don't think. Don't feel. Just get through tonight. Don't let him get into your head and take anything else from you. You can fight again tomorrow.

It was a mantra she'd learned in therapy. That

one-day-at-a-time self-talk had gotten her through the worst moments of her life. She'd gone a couple months now without preaching the words of survival to herself. But she needed them tonight. She was supposed to be safe here in Kansas City. Safe in her own apartment. Safe in a new job where her past couldn't find her. This was supposed to be a new beginning. A new life.

Allison Tate didn't scare easily.

But she was scared now.

"Payback" had awakened a whole hell of a lot of fear in her tonight.

Stay busy.

Allie scooped up Gray's bag from beside the front door and carried it into his bedroom where she laid it and the crutches she didn't think he truly needed across the foot of the bed. The clean laundry piled there demanded she take the time to fold it and stack it neatly in the basket. There it was again. Gray's scent. Distracting her. Clinging faintly to the towels she folded, even after a trip through the wash. She buried her nose in the soft, cotton terrycloth, and imagined the cool, fresh scent came from his shampoo or shower gel. She imagined it in his short, crisp hair. On his skin.

It was an irresistibly manly smell, a soothing smell. She didn't need to stress. She was safe here in Gray's apartment. Gray made her feel safe.

No. Gray made her *tingle.*

Allie's eyes popped open at the silent admission. Being attracted to a man right now was so not safe. Grayson Malone had his own demons to fight. He didn't need her issues dumped on top of his. She should go. But that was an irrational response. She'd stood her ground and fought the last time her life had turned upside down. She was a trained Navy lieutenant. She was physically stronger now than she'd been two years ago, thanks to all the running and defense training she did. She was more stubborn than any of the patients she dealt with. Besides, where would she go? Home to her parents? And possibly put them in danger? Bunk on a friend's couch? Who were her friends in Kansas City? Whom could she trust to handle the kind of trouble she'd be bringing with her?

Doug Friesen? She snorted through her nose at the idea of trusting that man with anything.

Maeve Phillips? No, she wouldn't subject her young coworker to this kind of threat.

One of the men she'd gone out with? There was a reason she hadn't agreed to a second date with any of them.

Ivy Burroughs? Although they chatted and worked together several times a week, the sweet older woman was a patient, not a friend.

Someone from her last duty station back in Jacksonville? Hardly. The people she'd called friends there had distanced themselves and left her to fight her battle on her own.

There was only one name on her list of trusted friends now.

Grayson Malone.

Handsome green eyes and short, high and tight hair she itched to run her palms over flashed through her mind. Did she really want to drag him into her troubles and use him as an ally?

Allie cursed. This wasn't fair! Why couldn't she enjoy a few lusty impulses with her Marine-next-door crush? Why couldn't she get the answers she needed tonight? She wanted to go back home and continue playing her flirty little games, trying to get Gray to wake up and notice her as something more than a friend. But she was afraid to go home now. To be alone. Why did she have to be afraid?

Because she knew just how bad things could get when she had no allies. No backup. No safe place to land.

Don't think.

Allie shook off the downward spiral of her thoughts and looked for another distraction. Gray's bedroom was as masculine and sparsely furnished as hers was feminine and full of pictures and meaningful tchotchkes from family and friends. Was his lack of decor a bachelor thing? A conscious, clutter-free choice that made life in a wheelchair or walking on fake legs easier? Then why let the dishes overflow the kitchen sink? Did he not have family and friends and good memories to fill up the empty spaces in his life? She wanted to give that man a hug. She wanted to dance with him again. She wanted to make memories with him that would bring smiles and colors and stories to his life.

Stay busy.

Finding the linen closet in the master bathroom, Allie gathered the armload of towels and set them inside. The hints of Grayson's scent she found so mesmerizing increased tenfold in the small room. She lingered in the doorway and breathed in the scents she associated with Gray until she started to feel a bit like a creeper. Heaven help her, she wanted to curl up in that scent and be surrounded by it.

Don't feel.

Moving on, she gave herself a tour of his spare bedroom, which he'd set up as a home gym, perused the books and Blu-ray collection stored in his entertainment center around a flat-screen TV, plumped the cushions on his sectional sofa—the only other piece of furniture in the living room—and finally returned to the kitchen. With nothing left to do to pass the time, Allie tested her now cold food and reheated their meal from the Chinese restaurant. She found a second plate for Gray and set the table for a really late dinner.

She forced down a bite of soggy egg roll while pushing the rice around on her plate. She was about to toss the whole thing into the trash when she heard the key turn in the door lock.

Logic told her no one but Grayson could be coming into his apartment. But raw nerves and wary survival instincts had her reaching across the table for the steak knife. Once she saw his broad shoulders and familiar green eyes, she eased her grip on the knife's wood handle. "Is your team finished with my apartment?" She pushed her chair back and stood. "I'll get out of your way."

"Sit, Allie." Gray's weary gaze locked on to her hand, but he made no comment about arming herself. "You can relax for now. At least, finish your food." He bolted the door behind him and rolled his chair through the apartment. "My team will take the evidence we gathered back to the lab and start processing it in the morning. Your place is taped off, and there's an officer stationed outside."

"Sounds secure enough."

"Not safe enough for you to be sleeping there," Gray insisted. "Besides preserving the crime scene, there's the risk of contaminants from all that blood. Lexi is already putting together a list of volunteers to come over to clean up and repaint anything we need to once the scene is released."

"You and your friends don't have to do that."

"It's done." He washed his hands as he continued. "It's not good for your mental health to be surrounded by reminders like that. Take it from someone who knows a little bit about recovering from trauma. Eventually, you'll have to face it again." He grabbed a towel and dried his hands. "But not tonight. Some time and distance can help you rebuild your strength and cope with the aftereffects." He hooked the towel over the edge of the sink before facing her again. "I have a feeling you already know that, though."

"I just need answers. An explanation. Then I can move on." *Stay busy.* Allie pulled his dinner from the microwave and set it on the table. "You must be starving. Here."

He tilted his face to hers, refusing to take a bite until she sat and picked up her fork again. Once she swallowed a mouthful, he dug into his cashew chicken. Between bites, Gray reached into the pocket of his sweats and set her mailbox key on top of the table. "There were no signs that your spare had been removed—no minute shavings to indicate it had been through a key cutter, either."

"How did he get into my apartment?" Allie dropped the key into her purse hanging over the back of the chair.

"That's the million-dollar question. My best guess is he somehow got a copy of your key while you were at work. Or some other place where you lost track of it."

"I don't lose—"

"You don't lose track of your keys. Just like you never forget to lock the door."

"I'm a woman alone in the city. I'm always careful," she insisted.

Allie shivered. Clearly, she'd slipped somewhere along the way. At least, someone wanted her to think she hadn't been as diligent as she should have been.

"Maybe they weren't with me twenty-four seven." Allie reached into the pocket of Gray's hoodie and pulled out her ring of keys. "How can you tell if it has been copied?"

Being careful to touch only the edges, Gray inspected the key. Then he pushed away from the table and rolled over to what turned out to be a junk drawer. He tore off two long pieces of scotch tape and stuck one to each flat side of the key. He studied it carefully under the bright light above the sink, then gently peeled off each piece of tape and inspected them, as well. Allie was curious enough to find out what he was seeing that she joined him at the sink. She braced a hand on his shoulder and leaned over him to see the results he pointed out. "I only see one thumbprint—yours, I'm sure. No trace of metal dust. If a copy was made, it doesn't look like it was from this one. Or it wasn't done recently. Any trace is long gone."

Although she liked seeing how focused, thorough and resourceful he could be, Allie wasn't thrilled with Gray's answer. "You think someone's been planning that break-in for a long time? Stalking me to be there if I lost track of my keys? Or distracting me so that someone else could gain access to them?"

He tossed the tape in the drawer and returned her

keys. "I deal in facts, not supposition. If it means anything, I don't think you made a mistake. I'm not sure how the perp got into your apartment, but this isn't on you. This was a highly planned attack. We'll figure it out."

"Of course. Thank you." When she tucked the keys into her pocket, she realized she still wore the hoodie Gray had loaned her hours earlier. She unzipped the jacket. "I forgot I had this on. I suppose you'll want it back."

"No." He wrapped his hand around her forearm, stopping her from shrugging out of the hoodie.

"No?"

"If you're cold and need it to stay warm, you're welcome to it."

"I don't want to take advantage—"

"You're not taking advantage of me, Allie. Your home was violated. You're second-guessing whether or not you could have prevented the break-in. If wearing my old hoodie makes you feel better, it's the least I can do to give you some comfort tonight."

He gently squeezed her arm before releasing her, and Allie wondered if he was aware of just how much they'd touched each other today. She certainly was aware. With every touch—as impersonal as his strong hands keeping her from falling, or as intimate as her fingers gently clasped in his as they danced—she felt a buzzing like fizzy soda dancing across her skin, leaving bubbles of warmth in their wake.

Tingling and dancing bubbles. Where were these romantic notions coming from? She'd always liked Gray. They had a lot in common—a shared military background, working together at the clinic, living in the same building and knowing a lot of the same people. But events tonight seemed to have knocked down whatever walls of professional detachment and self-reliance she'd kept between them, and she was *very* aware of the man. Not the neighbor. Not the friend. The man.

She hugged the hoodie more tightly around her and realized she was falling hard and fast for the Marine next door. This jacket smelled like him. Yeah, it made her feel better. Its warm, oversize bulk made her think he was holding her in his arms. She should be distancing herself from him, but she wasn't strong enough to do that right now. But it wasn't in her to lie about her feelings. "Gray, you've given me more comfort than you know tonight," she admitted. He paused midbite, frowning in confusion as she sat across from him. "You might want to rethink that 'taking advantage' thing, though. You said to make myself at home, and I did."

"You washed the dishes. I appreciate that." He glanced over to the counter. "The sink is a little high for me to be comfortable, so I usually put off that chore until there's nothing left to cook in."

"It wouldn't be too high if you wore your prostheses. And you wouldn't need your crutches here."

When his eyes narrowed at her opinion that he wasn't as broken as he seemed to think he was, she hurried to change the subject. "Full disclosure. I went through *all* of your apartment. I needed to keep busy. And, I was curious. It was...a distraction. Sorry I invaded your personal space."

"I've got nothing to hide from you." For a moment, he studied her as intently as he had her key. Then the corner of his mouth crooked up. "Did you roll around on my bed and mess it up?"

"No. But I folded the laundry that was there."

"Put things away where I won't find them?"

"I don't think so."

"Did you move the bookmark in the book I was reading?"

"No."

He pointed his fork at her and grinned. "I know. You threw out my girlie magazines."

"I didn't find any... Oh." Allie sat back, shaking her head. "You're teasing me. I didn't think you did teasing."

"I didn't think I did anymore, either." She wondered why that confession seemed to surprise him. He stuffed a forkful of food into his mouth. "You have a beautiful smile. You don't use it often enough."

Allie's cheeks warmed at the compliment. This unexpectedly fun side of Grayson Malone interrupted the malaise of her thoughts, giving her a momentary reprieve from her nightmarish fears.

She gave the teasing right back. "Practice what you preach, Captain Grumpy Butt."

He reached across the table and picked up her fork, encouraging her to eat. "I invited you here. I told you to make yourself at home. I wanted to give you a respite from all that crap you had to deal with next door."

"I'm used to dealing with anything that comes up on my own." She stabbed a snow pea. "I'm also *not* used to letting things get under my skin like this."

"I suspected as much. Think of it as a favor from one veteran to another. Letting you hang out here, touching my stuff, looking through all my things—"

"I didn't look through all—"

"—is me having your six."

"My six?" Allie inhaled a deep breath and nodded. Yeah. Knowing someone had her back right now felt good. "I haven't heard that phrase for a while. I was never in combat, but we dealt with enough of the aftermath in the hospital and therapy clinic that I appreciate being part of a team." Knowing someone she trusted had her back was the thing she'd missed the most when her life had gone south back in Jacksonville. She'd had no one to plan a survival strategy with, no one to give her a respite when she needed a break from all the stress, no one to still be her friend when she became a pariah. Allie swallowed the pea pod and speared another. They ate for a few minutes in silence before she asked, "Are the police done asking me questions?"

"For tonight."

"And your crime lab teammates are gone?"

Gray nodded.

"Am I allowed to go back in there and pack a bag? FYI, you didn't have to warn me off. I don't intend to stay there until Bubba can get the locks changed. But I would like to check into a hotel before it gets too late."

"You really want to stay alone in a hotel room?" Gray polished off the last of his meal. "It's late and you're exhausted. Crash here tonight and we'll figure out the next step in the morning. The officer will escort you inside your place if you want to grab some toiletries and pack an overnight bag. Or you can use what I have here." He gathered his utensils, picking up the steak knife, too. "Officer Chambers will keep an eye on my place, too. You don't need to sleep with this. No one will get to you here tonight."

Of course, he hadn't missed that she'd been ready to defend herself against whoever came in that front door. "Thanks. But I already told you, I searched every room. You don't have an extra bed."

Gray nodded over his shoulder. "The sectional is a comfortable place to sleep. I've crashed there many nights, after staying up too late watching a movie or ball game. You can take my bed."

"If the sectional is so great, I'll take it," Allie insisted. "All I need is a pillow and a blanket."

"Deal." He cleared the table around her, encouraging her to continue eating. "Why did you check on the location of a known felon?"

"How did you know that was what I was doing?" Maybe Grayson Malone was a little *too* smart for her. Allie tossed her fork onto her plate and pushed it away. "There goes what little appetite I had left."

"I can fix you something else. Sandwich? An omelet?"

Carrying her plate to the sink, Allie shook her head. "I'm good."

"You said you were hungry earlier. You need to keep up your strength. I have ice cream."

The man didn't miss a detail—she'd mentioned her love for ice cream at the clinic. But the thought of putting any other food in her stomach right now was worse than skipping a meal altogether. "You wouldn't have a cup of tea, would you?"

"Sorry. I'm a coffee guy."

"Maybe just some water?" She turned on the faucet to rinse their plates.

But Gray reached around her to turn it off. He tugged on her wrist and turned her to face him. "Enough stalling. While I appreciate the help, you are not my maid." Even though he had to tilt his head to hold her gaze, because his upper body was so long and his shoulders so broad, he made her feel surrounded by him. "Are you going to answer my question about NAVCONBRIG CHASN, or are you going to make me find the connections for myself?"

Allie looked down into his handsome green eyes, then had to look away—had to pull away because the intensity of those eyes seemed to pierce right into the heart of her. She headed into the living room and settled on the edge of his sectional couch. "I know you need me to talk about this. But I don't want to. The criminalist needs to hear the facts." She hugged her arms around her waist and buried her nose inside the collar of his jacket, breathing in the scent she was beginning to crave. "But I'm not sure I want my friend to know."

"Nothing you tell me is going to change the way I feel about you." He had feelings about her? Probably friendship. Maybe a sense of camaraderie since they'd both served in the military. Maybe gratitude since she didn't let him cut any corners when it came to his physical therapy and healing. She heard him moving behind her. "To be honest, it's a relief to know that I'm not the only one facing a problem that seems too big to surmount."

"You're glad my apartment was vandalized?"

He rolled his chair around the end of the couch and handed her a bottle of water from the fridge. "That didn't come out right. Someone threatening you doesn't make me feel better. But it gives me something to focus on besides wallowing in my own self-pity."

"You have nothing to feel self-pity about."

He slapped his thigh. "Missing my legs, my buddies from my unit and the self-confidence I used to wear like a second skin when it comes to anything outside of work?"

"Grayson—"

"Talk to me, Lieutenant. Distract me." He dismissed her argument without giving her a chance to think about shoulders and scents, teasing, dancing, hand-holding and unexpected tingling.

"You sound a little bossy to be doubting that self-confidence of yours."

This time, the teasing wasn't going to work for either of them. "Tell me first. It'll be easier to tell Officer Cutler later."

She pulled the sleeves of the hoodie down over her fingers. "I don't want you to see me as a helpless, fragile female."

He looked at her as though she'd spoken gibberish he couldn't understand. "Fragile?" He surprised her, reaching out to grasp the tab of her zipper, and cinched the jacket closed beneath her chin, tucking her into its warmth. "Maybe for about two seconds tonight. But you're entitled. Feminine? Always. Being tough with your patients and keeping yourself in fighting shape doesn't change that. And *helpless* is the last word I would ever associate with you."

He captured both of her hands and gently chuffed them between his. Resting his elbows on his knees, he leaned toward her. "Your hands weren't this cold when I held them at the clinic this evening. Confirms my theory that you're pretty shaken up about what happened tonight. But you didn't run screaming out of your apartment or collapse in a pile of tears. You armed yourself with pepper spray and reentered the premises with me."

"I felt safer with you."

"You remembered your training. You kept your head despite your fear. Nothing you've done tonight makes me think you're weak or helpless." His nostrils flared as he inhaled a deep breath. "Accepting help does not mean you're helpless."

"Something your therapist said to you?"

He grinned. "Something my *physical* therapist said to me."

Allie wanted to answer that wry smile, but she couldn't. Not if she was going to talk about her past. Time to practice what she preached.

"Chances are, I could outrun or fight off a threat that was pursuing me." Her grip pulsed within his. "But to have some unseen enemy sneaking around me, messing with my things, watching me—and I didn't even know the threat was still there? That unnerves me a little bit."

"'Still?'" Was there any detail this man missed? Gray went on. "It gets in your head. Makes you doubt yourself. You want to put a name to that threat and take care of it. I'm guessing that name has something to do with a Navy prison." When she would have pulled away, he tightened his grip. "I already have Chelsea O'Brien, our crime lab computer guru, on standby to look up any threats you have lurking in your past. But if I knew how to direct her search, we'd get answers a lot faster." His eyes demanded her gaze. "Why do you have a prison number on speed dial?"

Allie could see the men in Gray's platoon obeying that stern, narrowed gaze.

She could see women responding to the intense maleness of it. It made even an Amazon warrior like her feel like she was womanly, cared for, protected.

"I was checking on the status of a prisoner. Making sure he was still incarcerated there. I want to make sure he hasn't escaped or been paroled for good behavior—which he could totally fake."

"Sounds a little like a sociopath. If he's out, you think he'll be coming for you?"

"He'd certainly want payback." Her gaze darted to the wall separating their two apartments before facing him again. "But the NCO on duty tonight couldn't help me. The base commander's office is closed until morning. I'm to call back after 0900 to confirm he's still locked up."

"If he's still there, it'd be a good idea to get this guy's visitors' log, too. He could have called in a favor or hired someone to terrorize you." Gray pulled his cell phone from the pocket of his sweats and typed in a text. But he looked up, seeking the answer to his unspoken question before he hit Send.

"Noah Boggs. The name you want to research is Noah Boggs. He was a doctor at the base hospital where I worked."

"Chelsea can find answers online that we mere mortals can't." He typed in the name Allie spelled out, sent the text, then set his phone aside. "Now, what's the *payback* for?"

"Could you…? Would you sit with me?"

"It's easier to talk about this if you don't have to look me in the eye?"

Oh, yes. Mr. Intensity was in crime-lab mode right now. This conversation would be easier if she had her neighbor/friend/crush to lean on, instead. "The body heat doesn't hurt, either."

"That's your reaction to stress? The blood stops circulating to your extremities, and you get cold?"

"Something like that. Please?"

A shadow dimmed the rich green of his eyes as his gaze dropped to the cushion beside her. Then he gave a curt nod, set the brake on his chair and easily pushed himself up onto his thighs like he had in her apartment. He flipped around and plopped down onto the sofa beside her. "Can't have you freezing on me. I don't have that many blankets in the house."

Again, she was struck by the size of the man.

Gray mistakenly thought his wheelchair or prosthetic limbs diminished his presence. But Grayson Malone overwhelmed her senses. Allie's forehead barely cleared his shoulder as he sat beside her. Sitting this close, she could see the individual hairs of the wheat-and-bronze stubble that shaded his jaw and neck. Even through the layers of shirt and scrubs and hoodie, she could feel the heat coming off his body. And yeah, there was the scent she would always associate with sexiness and security.

He fussed with the cotton jersey of his sweatpants, tucking the pinned folds beneath the end of his stumps and smoothing the material over his tree-trunk thighs.

Allie toed off her work clogs and curled her legs up beneath her. She purposely let her knees rest against Gray's thigh and pulled his left hand into her lap. "Relax. I won't bite. I promise."

Gray's laugh held little humor. "My last girlfriend didn't like my legs touching her. Freaked her out."

"Stupid woman."

Now, *that* was a real laugh.

"It's her loss." Allie wrapped both hands around Gray's and butted her arm against his, making sure he understood that his touch was exactly what she wanted. "You're a furnace. I like that about you."

He splayed his fingers, then laced them together with hers, holding her hand as tightly as she'd latched on to his. "All right, Lieutenant. No eye contact. A little body heat to warm you up. A kind boost to my ego. Enough stalling. Tell me about Noah Boggs."

"It's complicated. But basically, my testimony sent my ex-boyfriend—a fellow Naval officer—to prison."

"For what?"

Allie traced the length and strength of his fingers intertwined with hers. "We worked at the same hospital in Jacksonville. He launched a harassment campaign against me after I went out with him a few times and then decided we weren't going to be a good fit."

"Why not?"

"It was always about him. He was good-looking. Fun to flirt with. At first, I thought he was funny and kind. But if I wasn't in the mood to laugh or I didn't show enough appreciation, he got weird."

"'Weird' how?"

"He'd be critical. Demanding. He'd praise me with one sentence and put me down the next. Like, I was a strong woman. I could take whatever he dished out. I should learn from my mistakes and be even stronger."

"'Mistakes?'" Grayson growled a curse. "And anything that didn't stroke his ego or serve his needs was a mistake?"

Allie nodded. "I was late getting off work one time, and we were supposed to have dinner with the hospital administrator and her husband. He went without me so my tardiness wouldn't embarrass him.

Or, I kissed him wrong. I needed to let him control our physical contact." Gray's hand squeezed around hers. "I told him I wanted our relationship to be a partnership. There should be give as well as take. I wasn't there to be his verbal punching bag. I told him he was the only mistake I'd made, and that it wasn't going to work out between us."

"He didn't take rejection well?"

Understatement of the year. "He made a token effort to win me back, but I knew things would get worse, not better. I gave him a firm no."

"And that set off whatever landed him in prison?"

"We were both still in the Navy. He was completing his residency at the hospital where I worked in the physical therapy department. He commanded the patient treatment team we served on together. After I made it clear I wasn't playing hard to get, and we weren't getting together, he wrote me up for a couple of stupid infractions. Gave me crappy assignments. He'd say and do inappropriate things for a working relationship. I tried to distance myself, but he was always there."

"Like Friesen. That's why he gets under your skin when he hits on you at the clinic. It pushes a hot button for you."

"Imagine Doug with a mean streak. Doug is annoying and inappropriate, but Noah was…scary. I'd catch him watching me—at work. He'd check on a patient during one of my PT sessions, or be waiting in the hallway when I got out of a meeting. He parked outside my apartment, followed me to a restaurant. He isolated me from my coworkers and friends. He pulled rank on anyone who did stand up for me." Her gaze dropped to where their fingers were linked together. "After a while, no one stood up for me."

Gray released her hand to hug his arm around her bent knees and pulled them farther across his thigh, tucking her closer to his side. He folded his right hand around both her hands, this time pulling them into his lap. "Not going to happen anymore. Not with Boggs. Not with Friesen."

It was a comforting, warm embrace. Allie rested her cheek against Gray's shoulder and snuggled in. "I only had a year until I either had to re-up or leave the Navy. I thought I could ignore him and put up with it—until his games impacted one of my patients. He switched medications to make it look like I'd made the mistake. The patient had an allergic reaction and went into anaphylactic shock and nearly died. No one believed me at first when I reported him. He was part of an old boy network—officers protecting officers, that kind of thing. I kept documenting each incident with my superiors. A patient nearly dying wasn't something anyone could overlook. He was finally arrested and put away, based mostly on my testimony."

"Sounds like you've had combat experience, after

all," Gray whispered. "He's in prison for harassment? Malpractice?"

Allie was exhausted, her emotions spent. She wanted nothing more than to climb onto Grayson's lap and feel his arms wrap around her. Instead, she yawned against his sleeve and finished the story. "When I reported the incident with the patient, Noah received a reprimand in his file that cost him a promotion, and the JAG office set up a hearing about revocation of his commission. Noah was pretty pissed about his career imploding. Of course, he blamed me. And he…he tried to kill me."

Grayson's entire body tensed beneath her. Allie would have pulled away if she didn't feel the press of his lips against the crown of her hair.

"You aren't calling the prison at 0900." His words were husky. Terse. Her hair caught in the stubble of his beard. "I'll put Chelsea to work. She'll pull a complete profile for Boggs and give us a location on him. You won't have to talk to the prison again."

Although Allie felt as though a burden was being lifted from her shoulders, she was hesitant to surrender her independence. Standing up for herself was the one thing that had kept her safe, had kept her alive. "We're not in the military anymore, Gray. You can't tell me what to do."

"The hell I can't. Even if you do call Charleston, I'm getting the information through Chelsea. In the meantime, I'll be working the investigation from the scientific end of things. Solving problems is what we do. Let me help."

"I'm really tired. Tired of being on my own. Tired of fighting this. Just…tired."

"I know, babe." She felt his lips against her hair again. "If you trust me, close your eyes for a little while. I've got your six."

Grayson's scent surrounding her was the last thing Allie remembered as her eyelids drifted shut.

THE VISITOR SAT in the car parked in the shadows.

Interesting. Light glowed through the window shades of Grayson Malone's apartment. Even at this late hour, there was activity in his residence, while the lights in Allison Tate's apartment had never come back on once the police and CSI van had left the building.

The visit to the woman's apartment that afternoon had caused an even bigger stir than one could have hoped for. The wait had been worth it—gathering all the necessary intel, getting to know the right people, formulating a plan that would do the most damage, deliver the most pain, before justice was finally served. After losing so much, there would finally be vengeance.

Now that the plan was in action, things were moving more quickly than anticipated. And this twist—the veteran Marine and the Navy lieutenant spending the night together—was as unexpected as it was welcome.

The visitor snapped a photograph for the scrapbook before starting the engine. “I don’t get it. I must have struck a real tender nerve for you to be turning to him.”

And the Marine must be beside himself, trying to figure out how half a man like him was ever going to save the girl next door.

The driver in the car laughed before driving away into the night.

This was going to be so satisfying.

Chapter Five

Grayson looked up from the printout he'd been reading as his cell phone vibrated with an incoming text. He pulled the phone from the pocket of his lab coat and set it on the stainless-steel lab table where he was working. He smiled and shook his head. Who would have guessed that Allie Tate could be so chatty? Or that he was enjoying these messages they'd been sharing throughout the day? She must be texting him between patients. So far, they'd touched on everything from a reminder that she'd forgotten to leave his gray hoodie at his apartment before changing for work this morning to discussing favorite take-out places and what their best home-cooked specialties were—he was a simple steak-on-the-grill guy while she claimed to make some mean pasta dishes.

He was grinning with anticipation as he typed in the unlock code and pulled up her latest text.

Mind if we do another sleepover? Officer Cutler just called to let me know I have full access to my apartment again. But I'm not ready to face the mess yet. Maybe after this weekend. I'll have more time to clean/paint/burn it down so it feels like home again.

A second text quickly followed the first.

Or, there's a hotel close to the clinic. I can make a reservation there. I don't want to overstay my welcome.

Gray typed in his response. She wasn't staying by herself in a hotel. She wasn't staying by herself anywhere. She was keeping the damn hoodie if it kept her warm, and she was staying with him.

Allie claimed she didn't have many friends in Kansas City yet, and her parents were teachers in a small town more than two hours away in central Missouri. She'd severed ties with her former military friends and coworkers who'd let her down so royally after Noah Boggs had targeted her for retribution. She didn't have anyone to lean on—not that she was used to doing that. But she had him. And Gray wasn't about to let her down.

My sofa works just fine.

He spun his chair away from the equipment at his station and rolled over to the desk near his workstation. There was still work to do on the "Payback" case, as the crime lab's director, Mac Taylor, had dubbed the break-in at Allie's apartment at this morning's staff meeting. It had been a challenge for Gray to separate the blood samples he'd taken, simply because there were so many of them. Thus far, they'd all come from human donors. He'd already identified seven of the eight blood types, including those with positive and negative Rh factors. But it would take much longer to name the source of individual samples through DNA, if they were in the system, along with the trace substances he'd found in the blood. And that was if the trace substances hadn't contaminated the identifying elements in the samples.

His mind automatically went back to the Jamie Kleinschmidt case. Gray had identified the same embalming fluid that had preserved each jar of blood. But because of the toxic substance, several of the samples had degraded to the point that they couldn't build a conclusive DNA profile, and some of Kleinschmidt's victims remained unidentified to this day, as a result. If Gray didn't know his criminal history, he might think Kleinschmidt had something to do with this case. But Jamie Kleinschmidt hadn't fared well in prison, and he had hanged himself in his cell barely two years into his sentence. Another logical supposition was that they had a copycat serial killer on their hands. But why target Allie? She was relatively new to KC and civilian life. What could a blood collector be seeking payback for from her?

That took him back to her military connections.

After listening to the details of the hell her last year in the Navy had been, Gray wanted to ram his fist through Noah Boggs's face for the pain he'd put Allie through. He'd never met the man, or even seen a picture of him yet, but he knew Boggs would be a pretty boy. Handsome. Entitled. Full of himself. He'd love to break the doctor's pretty nose and let him know in no uncertain terms that he'd have the wrath of the Marine Corps coming after him if he so much as looked sideways at Allie again.

Gray's nostrils flared as he inhaled a deep breath and exhaled that wildly emotional response to the man who'd hurt Allie. He was just now getting reacquainted with using his new legs again—he wasn't ready to put his fist through anybody's face. But he could still feel those protective urges pricking beneath his skin. Allie Tate was a strong, funny, beautiful woman—and Noah Boggs had tried to break her because she'd stood up to him and done the right thing when no one else would. She'd sacrificed her Navy career, her relationships and her ability to trust.

Now she was his…

His neighbor. His physical therapist. His friend, Gray amended.

He didn't know why Allie had turned to him for help, but she had. And he wasn't going to let her down. He didn't need to be the big, lean fighting machine he'd been in the Corps to help her. He needed to listen and be there for her. He needed to be the smart guy at the crime lab and figure this out so that she'd feel safe. Allie needed answers more than she needed a champion to stand between her and the enemy.

So, answers she would get.

Setting aside his turbulent thoughts, Grayson pulled up the screen on his laptop to jot his findings in his report and map out the follow-up tests he and others needed to make. He'd ask Lexi to put Khari Thomas to work on the DNA profiling while he continued identifying the number of blood donors. He'd give Chelsea O'Brien, the crime lab's resident computer geek and queen of all things online, the job of tracking potential sources of that much blood. If he couldn't identify the non-biological components of the blood paint, Gray would get one of the crime lab's chemists to concentrate on that. Finding out what the evidence was made of could lead to finding out where the evidence had come from, which, in turn, could lead them to a suspect who had access to that evidence—like Jamie Kleinschmidt who'd worked a part-time job at a funeral home, where he'd gotten the embalming chemicals he'd used with his victims' blood.

Noah Boggs was a doctor, albeit one who'd lost his license to practice medicine. But he probably had the knowledge and connections to put together yesterday's break-in and vandalism. If Gray's research couldn't tie the blood samples to Boggs, he hoped he could tie them to the man's accomplice.

Aka, answers.

Gray's phone vibrated on his desk. He pulled up Allie's response to his invitation to stay the night at his place.

Whew! One less thing to worry about today. Thanks! I promise not to fall asleep on you and drool on you this time.

Funny. He'd liked the way Allie had curled her body into his and gone slack against his side as mental exhaustion and the late hour had claimed her. Allison Tate was a toucher—her head on his shoulder, her thighs butting against his, her hands interlinked with his. Without hesitation. Without making him feel self-conscious about his legs. Last night, she'd burrowed into him, held on tight, relaxed against him enough to fall into a hard sleep—as if his body was better than any bed he could offer.

In fact, he'd sat there a good half hour after he heard the first soft snore because it felt so good to cuddle with a woman again. He felt more like a man with Allie sleeping beside him than he ever had making love to his ex-girlfriend.

Brittany had barely been able to look him in the eye when he'd come home from the hospital, and she hadn't been able to mask her shock and pity when she saw his legs, even though she'd tried valiantly a couple of times to help him change his dressings or massage in some therapeutic skin cream. He'd been able to feel the stiffness in her when he hugged or kissed her. She'd wanted to be with the old Grayson Malone—Marine Corps veteran, war hero. But the 2.0 version was a harder man to love, to be herself with, to love as freely as she once had. And it wasn't just the legs. Grayson had been in shock himself, getting acquainted with his new body, relearning his new normal. He'd been fighting not to let the grief and anger over all he had lost color his relationship with Brittany. But it had. He'd become a lot of work to love.

No wonder she'd left him.

Allie was made of stronger stuff. She'd seen more of the world—dealt with a hell of a lot more danger and conflict—than Brittany had ever had to. And Gray was in a better place mentally now. Not all charm and confidence anymore—but not full of rage and fear, either. A woman like Allie could handle him on his worst day. She challenged him. Called him on his excuses and self-doubts. And, apparently, she needed him in a way Brittany never had.

He typed in a reassuring response.

You had a tough night. Drool just means you finally relaxed. I know how to do a load of laundry.

He could almost hear Allie's laugh.

We really need to work on your sweet-talking skills, Malone. You do not agree when a woman admits to drooling.

So, I shouldn't tell you that you snore, either?

Just wait until you're asleep, Malone. I'm bringing in a whole film crew to record your embarrassing habits.

"Knock, knock." Gray hit Send on a laughing emoticon before he looked up from his phone to see Chelsea O'Brien walk into the lab with her arms hugged around her laptop and a stack of file folders. She set them all on the corner of his desk before handing him the top folder. "Hey, Grayson, I've got some intel for you."

He opened the folder and studied both the prison mug shots and last Navy dress uniform picture taken of Noah Boggs. He knew it. The man had a pretty face. Gray's fingers curled into a fist with the urge to wipe that smug look off his Allie-hating expression. *Answers, Malone.* His job was to collect all the facts and let Officer Cutler and KCPD do their job—not to inflict retribution. He forced his grip to relax. "Is this everything I wanted to know about my suspect?"

"And more." Chelsea frowned behind her glasses—decorated with daisies for spring, he supposed—perhaps reading the protective anger coursing through him. "I can confirm that Boggs is incarcerated and hasn't left the military prison in Charleston for any reason since his sentence began. He isn't even scheduled for a parole hearing for three years. That dossier includes his service record, as well as a link to transcripts of the trial. Or admiral's mast. Or whatever it's called."

Gray thumbed through the pages of medical school transcripts, military police reports and more. Allie had done her job, reporting both medical and military infractions. As grim as last night's account of Boggs's harassment campaign against her had been, he could see she'd glossed over some of the details that would have made him lose his mind—like Dr. Boggs's final effort to silence Allie by tampering with her car and forcing her off a bridge into an accident that was meant to kill her.

Gray quickly closed the file and concentrated on a logical, rather than emotional, response to Chelsea's report.

"You remember the Jamie Kleinschmidt case?"

"Not the question I thought you'd ask." Chelsea hugged her arms around her waist and shivered dramatically from head to toe. "The one with all the blood in the basement?"

Gray nodded. "Where does someone get a lot of different types of blood—unless he's a serial killer who collects it?"

"Is this a creepy rhetorical question, or are you asking me to do some research?"

"Research." Gray jotted a note on a sticky pad. "I'm going to pull some old case files, see if anything pops for me. But if you can track down thefts from blood banks, hospitals, clinics—even a series of insignificant losses—or tainted or expired blood that's been disposed of—"

"Okay. Enough grossing me out." Chelsea had her hands up now, waving aside any further suggestions. "I don't like it, but I get the picture. I'm looking for someone amassing a large enough quantity of blood to paint your girlfriend's apartment."

"Allie's not my girlfriend."

"If you say so." Chelsea nodded to the phone on the lab table. "But I've never seen you text a woman—well, anyone—as much as you've been on your phone today."

"You spying on me?" he teased, making light of the fact someone else could see his interest in Allie.

"It's tech. It draws me like a magnet. Besides, you smile when you see who the message is from. You were grinning from ear to ear when I came in." She flipped her long brown braid behind her back and smiled indulgently. "And you don't smile often."

"Allie said the same thing."

"She knows you well, then. I think I like her."

He did, too. Despite his better judgment about getting involved with anyone after his disastrous breakup with Brittany. Gray pictured Allie falling asleep on the sofa, curled up against his side.

He could still remember her heat seeping into him through their clothes. He'd sat there with her for thirty minutes, trading warmth and inhaling her scent, before he laid her down and covered her with a blanket. Allie possessed a strong outer shell, which he admired. Yet he'd discovered she was achingly vulnerable when she let her guard down. The fact that she'd let him see that vulnerable side last night felt like sharing a secret. He was honored, humbled and more than protective to be on such intimate terms with her.

Yet he was scared that even if the attraction was mutual, which he was beginning to suspect was the case, that he'd let her down—that he might not be everything she needed. He hadn't been enough for Brittany, in the end.

"Why don't you make her your plus-one for Buck's and my wedding?" Chelsea's invitation snapped him from his thoughts, surprising him.

Her light, happy tone reminded him that other people found their happily-ever-afters, even if he couldn't. Gray was genuinely happy for his self-avowed geeky friend and the ex-cop who worked as a consultant for the crime lab. "You and the old man finally set a date?"

"One, Buck is not old. The man's got moves. He could dance circles around you."

He tapped his thigh. "Anyone could."

She made a face at his disparaging joke. But it got

him to thinking about Allie and her insistence that dancing would be excellent therapy for his balance issues. Maybe dancing wouldn't be such a bad thing if Allie was the woman he was holding in his arms.

"You know what I mean."

"I know," he assured her.

"And two, yes, we set a date for the fall."

"Congratulations." Gray reached out and traded a light hug with his coworker. "You and Buck are the oddest couple I've ever known. But you bring out the best in each other. I'm happy for you."

"Thanks. I offered to elope to Vegas whenever Buck wanted to, but he insisted I have a ceremony and reception with all the bells and whistles since I never had any big family events growing up. I think he likes to spoil me." Buck was a veteran cop and security expert, as tough as a bulldog and as much of a man's man as Gray had ever met. But he was an overprotective marshmallow—Chelsea's words—when it came to the woman he loved. Gray was glad for the reprieve in discussing his feelings for Allie. Not that he could have stopped Chelsea, anyway. The woman did love to talk when she got on to a subject that interested her. "My dogs are going to be our ring bearers. Buck's son will be the best man, and I asked my friend Vinnie from the Sin City Bar to give me away since he's like a grandfather to me. Lexi is going to return the favor and be my matron of honor. I'm inviting all my friends here at the lab, of course. You guys are my family now." She adjusted her glasses on the bridge of her nose and tilted her gaze to his. "And I'd like you, pseudo big brother, to be one of our ushers."

"Sounds like you've got it all planned out." She caught her bottom lip between her teeth, as if she expected him to say no. Gray wasn't about to disappoint her. "I'm honored you included me. I wouldn't miss it for the world."

"Great!" Chelsea jabbed a finger in his shoulder to get his attention before pointing to his mouth. "You'd better be wearing that smile when you come to the wedding. And save a dance for me."

"Will do."

She gathered up her laptop and files and turned to make her next information delivery. Gray stopped her before she reached the door. "Hey, Chels?"

"Hmm?" She turned.

"When you had to testify against Dennis Hunt—after all the things he did to hurt you and intimidate you—how'd you do it?" He knew it was a difficult topic for her, but Gray also suspected Chelsea might have an insight to Allie's situation that he lacked. "How did you stand up on that witness stand and do the hard thing? I know it's a tough question."

"Wow. Um, actually, it's not." She hesitated for a moment before drumming up a tight, sympathetic smile. "I could do it because I had Buck in my corner. And my best friend, Lexi, who got Dennis arrested. Plus, I had all of you guys. My family. You were all there in the courtroom with me. I knew I had people who had my back." She inhaled a deep breath before crossing the lab and perching on the corner of Gray's desk. "Does this have something to do with Allie? You know how alone I used to be. All I had were my rescue pets. Until I met Buck, and all of you. If Allie is facing this break-in, and whoever is responsible for it, alone—don't let her. Be there for her. And not just as the guy who's working her case."

"I may not be the best man for her to depend—"

"That's bull."

Gray's eyes widened at her huffy protest. Then Chelsea blinked and her typical quizzical expression returned. "Look, I know I'm the flaky one around here. But I see things. I get vibes about people—good or bad. I knew Dennis was trouble—and I knew Buck was my safe place." She hugged her things in one arm and reached out to squeeze his hand. "I see how you've been today with all those texts. And Lexi told me Allie's staying with you. I get a really good vibe about her. You care about her. I've never met Allie, but I'm thinking she sees you as more than a crime lab chemist and blood spatter expert." She dropped her gaze to Gray's phone. "I get the feeling she likes you, too."

"Thanks." Gray nodded before releasing her. "Buck's a lucky man."

"And Allie's a lucky woman." Chelsea stood, waving off the personal conversation. "I sent everything I have on Noah Boggs to your inbox, including a list of visitors he's had in prison. He's a surprisingly popular guy. I'm still gathering the deets on who everyone is, and if they have any connection to Kansas City and Allison Tate." Interesting. A lot of visitors meant a lot of opportunities to get word out about a tall physical therapist with honey-blond hair, and to reignite a harassment campaign against her. "If you need anything else, let me know. In the meantime, I'll be on the trail of a blood collector. Ew." Chelsea's shiver shook from her shoulders to her feet before she exited the lab. "I can't believe I just said that out loud."

After the door closed behind her, Gray picked up his cell and texted Allie.

I've been thinking about what you said about dancing. You willing to work with me?

Nearly an hour passed before she responded, reminding him that they both had work they needed to get done. He had just finished reading Boggs's file in detail, and the email Chelsea had sent, when his phone dinged with an incoming text.

Anytime, Malone. Not much of a response. But he knew that toward the end of the day, when patients were getting off work and out of school, was her busiest time for appointments. That was why he was surprised when she texted again. Are you coming in today?

I'm not scheduled again until Friday when I'm driving. Remember?

I forgot. Gray frowned. The Allie Tate he knew didn't forget things. A few seconds later, she asked, Do you need a ride home?

Was she trying to create more time with him? Even if Chelsea's hypothesis was correct and Allie was interested in more than friendship, he'd expect her to be more direct than that. He reminded her of the schedule they'd discussed this morning.

Jackson is giving me a lift. I'll be there when you get in and get dinner started.

Could he drop you off at the clinic, instead? It's closer to your lab. Then I could drive us home.

These texts sounded almost cryptic compared to the teasing back and forth they'd shared earlier. But what was the underlying message here?

Is something wrong? Is Doug giving you grief? Need a boyfriend to warn him off? I can ask Jackson to come in with me. He can scare anybody.

Not funny. Jackson's not the one who made me feel safe last night.

The alarm finally went off in his head. The phantom pain in his legs urged him to stand and take action. He couldn't, of course. Grayson swore. You don't feel safe?

...

Hell. Why wasn't she answering him?

Allie?

Can you please come? There's something I need to show you. Besides, I'd like to see you sooner rather than later.

He'd like to see her, too. No, he *needed* to see her as soon as possible if something was wrong.

On my way.

Chapter Six

Stay busy. Don't think. Don't feel.

Hell. The chant wasn't working. The overly fragrant flowers were giving Allie a headache. Or maybe that was the tension of the past twenty-four hours throbbing at the base of her skull. Maybe it was the one-handed former Marine scowling in silence on the far side of the counter or the silver-haired socialite with the bad hip, heaving an overly dramatic sigh every couple of minutes despite her indulgent smile.

Or, it could be Douglas "Clueless" Friesen's inability to take a hint and stay out of her personal space that had finally pushed Allie's patience out the window and made her snap. "Back off, Doug."

Doug had led both Ben Hunter and Ivy Burroughs into the patient area, announcing their arrival for their appointments. At the same time. Then he'd followed her into the space between the two long storage and supply counters at the end of the open physical therapy floor. His brown eyes sparkled with humor, as if her burst of temper amused him. "All

I asked is if you needed my help. You don't have to jump down my throat. Take a break. I can handle this for you."

"I don't need you to handle anything for me." Allie glanced at her phone before stuffing it into the pocket of her scrubs jacket. No new messages from Grayson. Did he get stuck at the lab? Was he really on his way? Why did it feel like she was barely hanging on until she could see or hear from him again? She wasn't sure exactly when her neighbor had become so important to her—maybe he had been all along, but she'd ignored her longings out of respect for his nonverbal cues to keep things casual between them, as well as not wanting to endanger the inherent trust between a physical therapist and her patient.

But all that denial and patience had gone out the window the moment she'd opened her door to Noah Boggs's threats, and she'd been terrified of facing the enemy again. She'd tapped into every bit of her mental, emotional and physical strength to survive Noah the first time in Florida. She wasn't sure she had the strength left to beat that threat again without knowing—without trusting with her very soul—that she had someone on her side this time. Someone who believed she wasn't making anything up. Someone who let her fight her battles without taking over or demanding something in return for his help.

Despite his words last night, she wasn't sure that

Gray wanted the job of guarding her six. But he was the one her soul said she could trust.

Allie picked up the heavy, gilded porcelain vase that had been delivered to her at the clinic and moved the flowers to the back counter. But the stems and greenery were so tall that they didn't fit beneath the upper cabinets there. Dumping them in the trash would draw even more attention to the flowers she didn't want. With a huff of frustration, she carried the bouquet back to the end of the front counter. Looking at them made her a little queasy, but the patients would probably enjoy them. "I can do my job, Doug. I just need a few minutes to work the problem so I can fix this mix-up."

"Sometimes people make mistakes. Even you." Doug reached in front of her and dragged the appointment calendar in front of him. "I'll bail you out. Which patient do you want me to take off your hands?"

Allie looked down at the cell phone in her hand and wondered if her instinct to contact Gray had sounded panicked or desperate. She'd been trying to keep things fun and cool and casual so she wouldn't scare him off, when all she'd really wanted to type was, *Get your tight butt over here. I need you!*

Allie eyed the two patients who were waiting for her answer, then turned her back to the vase of flowers and gestured to the book. "I did not schedule Ivy and Ben to come in at the same time. These two need full-time supervision—her for safety and Ben to keep him on task."

Ben Hunter tugged on his long beard before scrubbing his hand over the top of his close-cropped, nearly shaved head. "Are we going to do this, or what?"

Ivy Burroughs wore a smile instead of a frown. The silver streaks in her dark hair were perfectly coiffed and sprayed into place to highlight the chin-length waves. She wore enough rings and bracelets that she clinked and clacked when she gestured with her hands. "Your flowers are beautiful, dear. I know you want to call your boyfriend and thank him, but I really do need to get my appointment started. I'm playing cards with my girlfriends tonight. That's why I requested the earlier time. I want to clean up and change before I go. You know, in case, I—" she pressed her fingers to her lips to mask an embarrassed giggle "—sweat."

"You didn't mention needing to come early yesterday, Ivy," Allie gently insisted. "I would have remembered."

"Oh, I'm sure I did, dear." She reached over to stroke her fingers along the gold lines of the vase. "Maybe you were a little distracted with your man problems. Did you two have a fight? Is that what the flowers are for? I know my flowers. These cost a pretty penny. My son is always so good about apologizing when he makes a mistake." One moment she was talking romance and caring, and the next, she was back to complaining through her practiced smile. "Cards are always the first and third Thursdays of the month."

"Yes, but you never needed the extra time..." Allie held up her phone and rested her palm on the appointment calendar on the countertop, pointing out both places where she recorded her schedule. "I write it down, so I don't overbook appointments." Yet there it was under her name at four o'clock. Benjamin Hunter *and* Ivy Burroughs. "I didn't write this. Look." She opened the calendar on her cell phone to show each of them. "I've got Ben at four, and Ivy at five."

"It's not a problem for me to switch," Ben offered. "I can wait in the lobby. I've got nowhere else to go."

"Stop that." Allie pointed a stern finger at him. "You are not a second-class patient here. We'll get this straightened out without you having to make a sacrifice."

"Time, dear." Ivy tapped the watch face on the engraved gold bangle she wore. "Let him make the sacrifice. I don't want to be late."

"Ivy, please. Every patient matters here." Allie's head was ready to explode when the door from the lobby swung open, and Gray rolled his chair into the PT room. His green eyes swept the room. The moment his gaze landed on her they were both moving.

The tension left her on a noisy breath, and she

leaned in to hug him. But his hand was out, reaching for hers, and poked her in the stomach. Then he spread his arms open as she extended her hand. Allie curled her fingers into her palm, retreating from the awkward meeting. She didn't get far. Gray's hand shot out to capture hers and he tugged until her thighs hit the side of his chair. His other hand slipped beneath her scrub jacket and settled at the small of her back to rub soothing circles that warmed her through her scrub top and athletic shirt.

"Talk to me," he ordered.

Allie gripped his hand between both of hers. It wasn't the full-body contact she wanted, with his reassuring scent filling up her head. But Gray was here. She'd asked and he'd come. Reluctantly or not, no one had stood up for her in Jacksonville. She focused on those green eyes, and she could breathe normally again. He gave her the reprieve she needed to think clearly for a few precious moments. She remembered that she was strong and capable. Allie nodded to the bouquet on the counter beside her. "Are those from you, by any chance?"

"No."

"Then I'm officially freaked out."

"You don't know who sent them?"

She shook her head. "Even if the timing wasn't suspect, I'm not a big fan of surprises."

"Obviously. She's been snippy with everyone all day." Why did it sound as if Doug was tattling on her? Was he jealous that she'd dashed to Gray's side and clung to him when she'd shrugged off Doug's touch? "I would think getting flowers would make you happy. Don't all women love that?"

"White roses and gardenias? It looks like a funeral bouquet. No, I don't love that. Plus, the coward didn't have guts enough to sign the card." Allie reached into the vase to pull the card out, being careful to touch only the edges as she showed it to Gray. "There's no message." Just *Allie* written in a loopy, decorative script. "This guy's got a knack for making one word sound like a threat." She pointed out the two red spots below her name. "And…is that blood?"

"My guess is yes, judging by the irregular shape of the drops. I'd have to test it." Gray pulled a plastic evidence bag from his pocket and had her drop the card inside. "You think these are from Boggs?"

"From Noah, or someone doing it for him."

"Who's Boggs?" Doug asked from somewhere behind her.

Allie ignored him. "I can't prove it. It's not his handwriting—it probably belongs to the clerk at the floral shop who put the bouquet together. But it feels like they're from him. It feels like before."

"Boggs sent you flowers before?" Gray pressed.

"Who is Boggs?" Doug forced himself into the conversation. "You got another guy you're stringing along somewhere?"

Allie whirled around. "Get out of my personal

space, Doug. Unless you sent those flowers, this has nothing to do with you."

"Lighten up, Al." Doug held his hands up to placate her. His charming smile was suddenly absent. "I didn't send you the stupid flowers. It could be a mistake by the florist, and they sent them to the wrong Allie."

"There's no mistake." Allie turned her attention back to Gray again. He understood the flowers were sent to terrorize her. "After I broke up with Noah, he sent a bouquet every day for a week, or delivered them himself. At home or at work. He apologized over and over and tried to win me back. Then he was pissed that I wasn't grateful, and he couldn't change my mind. And then…"

"And then the crazy stuff started happening."

She nodded, claiming his hand again. "I'm a daisies and sunflowers kind of woman—not all these fancy, stinky flowers. Honestly, they make my nose run. Bigger and more expensive was always better with Noah, no matter what I wanted. If he'd only listened. If the relationship wasn't always about him."

Gray nodded. "Daisies and sunflowers. I'll remember that."

"I'm just making a point. I don't need you to send me flowers."

The lobby door swung open again and Jackson strode into the therapy room. He must have let Gray out at the door before parking the car. He set Gray's bag and crutches on the floor beside his chair. "She okay?"

Several therapy sessions stopped as patients and staff alike noticed the overbuilt stranger with the prizefighter's face and unsmiling countenance. Allie immediately extended her hand to dispel some of the curious glances. "Hi, Jackson. Thanks for bringing Gray."

The big man's nod must be his code for *You're welcome* or *No problem* or *You're a pain in the butt, lady.* Who knew what he was thinking behind those ice-gray eyes that seemed to always be scanning his surroundings?

Gray held up the bagged card. Jackson took it and studied it front and back, the two men silently communicating some evidence-processing scenario. "Ask Chelsea to track down whoever put together the bouquet at Robin's Nest Floral. See if she can find out who ordered them. I'm guessing it was in cash, maybe even using a fake name. And ask the florist if he or she poked herself on one of the thorns, or if they can even tell us who filled out the card. I'll type the blood myself later."

Another nod. "You want me to see if I can get anything off the flowers?"

"Take them. Please." Allie picked up the vase and shoved it into Jackson's hands. "When you're done getting fingerprints or finding out who sent them, donate them to a hospital or retirement home. If they don't survive whatever tests you have to run, just toss them. I don't want them back. I don't want any of it back."

Doug leaned on the counter beside her. "You're throwing away the bouquet? You've got a secret admirer, Al. You should show a little appreciation."

They still had their audience. Ivy reached across the counter to pat Allie's hand. "Doug is right. You're being awfully rude to whoever sent those." She looked at Gray, as if she hadn't heard or didn't believe his denial about sending them. "You're hurting his feelings, I'm sure."

Ben Hunter swore under his breath. "Give it a rest, lady. She said she doesn't want them."

"I wasn't speaking to you, young man. My son would never talk to me like that, and he certainly wouldn't use that language."

Another voice entered the fray when Maeve Phillips joined them. "Hey. You guys need to lower your voices. Your arguing is upsetting the other patients." She shied away from Jackson, who stood head and shoulders above her. But when her gaze met Ben's perpetual scowl, she nervously tucked her short dark curls behind her ears. "Is there something wrong with the flowers?"

"They're evidence in an ongoing investigation," Gray explained.

"Oh." Maeve seemed reluctant to meet his gaze, as well. "Is everything okay?"

Allie reassured the younger woman. "It seems I might have an old boyfriend stalking me. I'm taking care of things right now. Sorry if I'm worrying anyone."

"Stalking?" Maeve reached across the counter to grasp Allie's arm. "You worry about staying safe. We can handle the gossip mill. Just keep it down if you want this conversation to stay private." Maeve whispered, "Every table and workstation has ears."

Allie squeezed Maeve's hand before she pulled away. "I'll make sure the drama stops. Thanks."

With a nod, Maeve returned to her patient at one of the tables. Ben watched her from the corner of his eye, then resolutely turned away. He plopped his arm with the hook on the counter and leaned in. "Can we get this show on the road?"

Jackson looked down at Gray, who simply nodded.

Allie had seen sailors on the same SEAL team communicate the way Gray and Jackson seemed to. Baffling as it was to her, something about their backgrounds and training put them on the same wavelength. Maybe it was a man thing. Or a crime lab thing. Accepting Gray's dismissal and assurance that he was no longer needed, Jackson tucked the vase under his arm and headed back to the lobby. "I'll keep you posted."

"I'd better see to my own patients," Doug announced. Now that his effort to swoop in and save the day for her had been usurped by Gray's arrival and the resurrection of her own backbone, he wasn't eager to hang around. "If you need me to bail you out, holler."

She wouldn't.

Ivy wasn't so easy to dismiss. Maybe it was her age or her social status as the widow of a high-ranking officer, but she expected to be catered to. She tapped her manicured nail on the countertop. "Allie. I won't be charged for this session if we miss it, will I?"

"You're not going to miss it, Ivy. And you won't be late for your card game."

With the reminder of the terror campaign she'd survived gone with Jackson's departure, and Gray parked at the end of the counter beside her, Allie felt her equilibrium returning. "Ben, you want to bike or do the treadmill today to warm up?"

"I prefer running."

"Good. Thank you." The military man seemed to handle the word of an officer—even though they were both civilians now—just fine. She'd need a softer approach for the older woman. "Ivy, why don't you put your purse and jewelry away in your locker. I'll get Ben started, then I'll be ready to work with you when you come back. I'll meet you at the recumbent bike."

"All right, dear." Appeased by the compromise, Ivy limped off to the changing room.

Allie pointed out the open treadmill to Ben. "Once Ivy is set with her warm-up, I'll be back to start the occupational therapy for your new hand. We'll practice household tasks again today. If I'm running long, I'll send someone else over to monitor your form and progress."

"Just don't send Sweetcheeks."

"Who?"

"Maeve." He rubbed his right hand over the hook on his left. "I scare her."

"I doubt that..." But she could see that Ben believed the younger woman was afraid to work with him. If so, she didn't believe it had anything to do with his disfigurement. They worked with several disabled veterans here. But the clock was ticking, and Allie didn't have time to point out how the grumpy personality Ben wore like a shield might be the thing that made shy Maeve uncomfortable around him. She opted for teasing, instead. "Fine. I'll send Doug over to help if I'm in the middle of something."

Ben snorted a laugh. "You don't want to be owing that guy any favors."

"No, I don't. So, get to it, Sergeant."

"Yes, ma'am." He eyed her hand resting on Gray's shoulder before leaving.

Allie squeezed Gray's shoulder as she circled around his chair to follow Ben. "You sure you don't mind hanging out?"

Gray caught her hand before she pulled away. "I

won't be just sitting and watching the clock. My PT told me I needed to get in more practice walking on my new prostheses instead of relying on the chair."

"She sounds like a smart woman."

"I think so." He reached for her other hand and pulled her to the front of his chair where her knees bumped against the end of his thigh. Although he quickly shifted his leg away, he didn't let go. "It seems like you've got everything under control now. But are you really okay?"

"You think because I texted an SOS that I..." Gray wasn't smiling at her effort to make light of his concern. Good grief, the man was going to make her cry if he didn't stop looking straight into her soul with that piercing gaze. "I just... I have a raging headache, and I guess I had a panic attack when I saw the flowers. My blood pressure spiked. My patience vanished. Everything hit all at once. I didn't get enough sleep, I feel drained after rehashing my history with you last night, and—"

"And you needed someone to have your six, so you could catch your breath and think for a minute." Yeah, exactly that. "It's okay to send me an SOS when you need backup."

"Good to know. I'd better get going."

"Not yet." When she started to pull away, his grip on her hands tightened. "Breathe in through your nose." She did. "And out through your mouth. Again." Gray's presence, his command, calmed her.

She did two more relaxing breaths with him before he smiled. “You got this, Lieutenant.”

Allie nodded. Gray’s strong hands, the understanding in his eyes, the fact that he was simply here because she needed him, meant more to her than the most expensive bouquet in the world. Obeying the impulse that surged through her, she cupped the stubbled side of his jaw and leaned down to kiss the corner of his mouth. The texture of his skin was sandpapery against her lips, the temperature was warm, and yeah, she caught a whiff of the crisp, icy scent that was all him before pulling away. “Thank you.”

Gray reached up to cup her cheek and jaw the same way she’d held on to him. For a split second, Allie held her breath, expecting him to repeat the same action she had, hoping he would. He brushed the pad of his thumb across her bottom lip, and she felt the friction from the caress all the way down to the tips of her breasts and deeper inside. But there was no kiss.

Instead, his shoulders lifted with a deep breath, and he literally backed his chair away from her. “Go. I’ll be around.”

Was he dismissing her gratitude? Embarrassed by the public display of affection? Was he self-conscious about being in a wheelchair and unsure how to handle the physical intimacies of a kiss when she stood a foot taller than him? Or was Gray simply fighting harder than she was to deny the chemistry between them?

No matter the reason, Allie tried to remember how grateful she felt to have him in her corner, and not feel dismissed. They were friends, after all. Allies. And for the next hour, she needed to focus on the challenge of her job, not feel rejected by the man who was coming to mean more to her with every passing moment.

Chapter Seven

An hour later, Ivy Burroughs hugged Allie and thanked her for a rejuvenating workout with the feel-good recovery of an electrode and heating pad massage. The older woman waved to Gray, who was walking up and down the stair platform on his prosthetic legs. He was talking on his cell phone, deep in what looked to be a serious conversation with periodic nods and terse replies. He doffed Ivy a polite, two-fingered salute and continued his conversation. Allie started to smile at how he barely used his hand on the railing to steady himself. The man was distracted with work and not thinking about using his new limbs—he was simply doing it.

Then Ivy butted her shoulder and whispered a weird comment that Allie suspected was supposed to be a compliment. "He's a handsome man when he's standing up."

"He's handsome all the time," Allie argued, feeling weary and irritated by the unsettling events of the day. She did not need this woman spoiling the spark of a good mood with her insensitive ignorance. "Why would you say something like that?"

Ivy waved aside Allie's defense with a jangle of rings and bracelets. "Oh, I didn't mean anything about Mr. Malone being a cripple, dear."

A cripple? Allie fumed. "Mrs. Burroughs, we have several disabled veterans who come to the clinic for PT. You really need to watch your words. They can be hurtful, and even undermine a patient's recovery."

The older woman continued on as if Allie hadn't spoken. "Your man came to your rescue today. And he's had his eyes on you nearly the entire time he's been here. You clearly mean the world to him. I was hoping I'd get a chance for you to meet my son. I'm sure he's here to pick me up by now. But I see where your heart lies. Hmm… I wonder if Maeve Phillips is seeing anyone." She tossed her purse over her shoulder and winked. "Don't let that Mr. Malone go."

How Ivy Burroughs managed to sashay out of the clinic with a cane and a limp, Allie didn't know. But she had the uncharitable thought that she was happy to see the demanding patient go.

She glanced over to see Ben Hunter back on the treadmill again, running off the stress of his session. The Army veteran had opened up a little bit, sharing how much he missed his K-9 partner who'd been killed by the same explosive device that had taken his hand. But the touchy-feely conversation, combined with his frustration at the precision training on his prosthesis, had clearly dredged up some unwanted emotions, and Allie had encouraged him to run to his heart's content, provided he didn't go past her fifteen-minute time limit or break the machine.

Allie looked up at the clock with a weary sigh. Ten minutes to go. Her gaze was instinctively drawn to Gray again, and her feet followed. She met him at the bottom of the three-step unit and tilted her face up, taking in just how tall Grayson Malone was. She liked looking up at a man for a change—liked looking up at this man. She felt her cheeks burn as she recalled Ivy's tacky comments. Standing in his faded USMC sweats and T-shirt, it wasn't obvious that his lower pant legs were filled with steel rods. But even if he wore shorts or sat in his wheelchair, he was a whole man to her. And as much as she loved him holding her hand, she could admit to herself that she wanted a lot more. If he'd stretched out beside her and slept with her last night on the couch, she wouldn't have protested. And if that touch of his thumb to her lips earlier had been a real kiss…

"Thanks, Chelsea. Good job. As usual." He ended the call and tucked his cell into the pocket of his sweatpants.

"Work?" she asked, anxious to know if he had any answers for her.

"I've got some preliminary results from our investigation." His forehead creased with an apologetic frown. "I can confirm that Noah Boggs is still incarcerated. Chelsea talked to the Judge Advocate

General's office in Charleston. He had the guards do a visual check to confirm that he's in his cell. She's combing through a copy of the visitors' log and phone records now to see who your ex has been in contact with recently."

It should have been comforting to learn that Noah wasn't here in Missouri. But that just meant he was working with someone, or that someone was copying his terror campaign—and that meant she had no clue who was tormenting her. "Has Chelsea found any connection to Kansas City yet?"

Gray shook his head. "Don't give up hope, Lieutenant. We're still going to find out who's doing this to you and put a stop to it." He released his grip on the railing and leaned toward her, as if to comfort her. But he wobbled a bit as his balance shifted, grabbed on to her shoulders to stop himself from falling and muttered a curse. "I'm such a smooth operator. I seem to grab you as much as Friesen does."

Allie reached up to wind her fingers around his wrists to maintain the connection. "You can hold on to me anytime, Malone. The difference is that you have my permission to touch."

"Yeah?"

"Yeah. I hope the permission is reciprocated, as well." With her thoughts already turned to needing and wanting, Allie moved one hand to the center of his chest and gently pushed his shoulders over his hips. "Remember to center yourself."

"This would be easier if I had at least one good

leg to rely on." He quickly righted himself without really needing her help.

But Allie didn't move her hand from the warmth of his skin through his cotton T-shirt. "Forget the legs. Rely on this." She patted his firm belly and felt him suck in his breath. "You've got more muscles than just about anyone here, including the staff. Your prostheses are fitted properly to your larger thighs now. Use the muscles you've already got. You're not going to walk like you did before. But you're still going to walk."

"And dance." Allie chuckled as he slid his hands down her arms. "You said that was the best therapy for me." He tucked his left hand beneath her jacket at her waist and captured her right hand in his. "Let's keep it to a slow waltz, though, okay?"

"Okay." Allie let her fingers settle at the side of his neck. They swayed back and forth in a silent two-step and even managed a three-point turn that made Allie proud. "That's it. You've got this."

"What did Mrs. Burroughs say that upset you?"

Allie didn't bother denying her reaction. But she did fudge a bit on the details. "She thinks you're handsome."

"And you disagree? You're jealous? I swear I'm not into women who are old enough to be my mother. Oh..." He read the meaning in her gaze dropping from his. The dance stopped. "She said I was handsome for a handicapped guy."

"Something like that."

"You don't have to defend me against rude comments from small-minded old women. They can't hurt me."

Allie's chin came up. "Well, it hurt me. No, it ticked me off. You're important to me." He didn't believe how attracted she was to him, and she had a feeling that careless, ignorant comments like Ivy's had a great deal to do with his inability to trust a woman's feelings for him—to trust *her* feelings. His ex, Brittany, had probably said something similar, not meaning to hurt him, but making him feel different or less. Making him doubt himself. "I stand up for the people and things I care about."

"Easy, Tate." Gray's hand tightened at the nip of her waist, pulling her back into the swaying rhythm that in no way matched the soft background music being piped into the clinic. "You'll stand up and say or do what you think is right, no matter what it costs you."

She nodded, urging him to move in a circle around the stair unit, challenging him to take bigger steps and control his balance. "I had to stand up to Noah. I couldn't let him hurt anybody else. I couldn't let him win."

"Have you taken up a new cause since moving to Kansas City?"

Other than obsessing over the criminalist next door? Allie shook her head. "Settle into the new job. Find the best running paths. Adapt to civilian life."

"Nothing worrisome in any of that," Gray agreed.

"So, what battle do you think he's trying to win this time?"

Allie shrugged. "'Payback?' I didn't provide the only evidence against him, but the JAG said my testimony is what got him convicted."

Gray's eyes narrowed with a deep thought. "He's still in prison. Trying to kill a patient, trying to kill you—he's going to be there for a while. Tormenting you doesn't change his situation."

"It probably gives him some emotional satisfaction." Allie had pondered Noah's motives, too. It all came down to his ego and punishing her for not worshipping the ground he walked on. "He's probably thinking, scare her. Give her an ulcer. Make it impossible for her to trust another man and move on with her life—maybe make it impossible to trust herself."

"I accept that hypothetical scenario. Hurting you makes him feel better. But what's his end game? Turn you into a recluse? Drive you crazy? Finally succeed in killing you?"

Allie stopped in her tracks. Although she was pleased to see that Gray maintained his upright posture at the abrupt halt, the dark turn of their conversation chilled her. "Well, you just took a perfectly nice dance and turned it into a trek down nightmare road. I thought you were flirting with me with the dancing and small talk, but you're working the case."

"Oh, I was definitely flirting with you. I'm just not very good at it. Totally out of practice."

Allie shoved her fingers into her hair, rubbing

at the base of her skull and tugging loose some of the strands from the top of her ponytail. But she couldn't seem to ease the tension there. "So, I can't read your signals, and you can't read mine. I guess we've both been hurt enough and share enough distrust that we'll have to come right out and say what we're feeling if we want to clue the other one in… And what are you getting at?"

"Noah Boggs is stuck in South Carolina. Who's doing the work for him in KC? It's not like his accomplice can call and give him a daily update. If no one is reporting to him regularly, then he doesn't benefit from terrorizing you. Who does?"

"I don't know. Maybe he's getting off on just imagining how scared I am. Does it have to make logical sense?"

"For me? Yeah." Gray reached out to capture one of the long strands of hair she'd pulled from its binding and brushed it back across her cheek to tuck it behind her ear. His fingertips dug into the knot of tension at the nape of her neck. Although she welcomed his touch, the topic didn't change. "We need to be looking at other people in your life. Who else in this world wants to hurt you? And is this going to culminate in someone else running you off the road and trying to kill you again? I don't even want to think about it. The perp has stolen a page out of Boggs's playbook because he knows those kinds of mind games will hurt you the most. I believe someone else is doing this."

Allie wanted to lean into the hand that cupped the side of her jaw and neck. No, she wanted to lean into that USMC logo over Gray's chest and really feel him hold her. She did neither. He was offering answers, not comfort. "It's not bad enough that one man wants to hurt me, ruin me, kill me? Now there's someone else out there I've really pissed off?" She hugged her arms around her waist and shrugged, dislodging his hand. "I don't have any idea who else could be behind these weird happenings. Much less why."

She smelled the sweat a split second before she heard Ben Hunter's voice behind her. "I'm in."

Startled by his sudden appearance when she'd last seen him across the room, Allie jumped and fell against Gray. To his credit, her crush-worthy neighbor remained upright and shifted her to his side, leaving his hand at the small of her back. "You're in what?"

"Whatever's going on here with Allie." Ben glanced at her but focused his unhappy glare on Grayson. "I'm going stir-crazy with no job and all these physical and mental attitude adjustments. Clearly, someone is screwing with your woman. Gossip runs freely here. I know about the break-in at her apartment. The blood. That the flowers are probably from an ex—or someone who wants her to think they are. I want to help. Give me something to do."

Your woman?

Before she could explain the details of her relationship with Gray, the two men were exchanging phone numbers. Since Gray wasn't making any effort to correct Ben, she fell silent and let him take command of the formerly enlisted man. "I'd like to have eyes on Allie when she's here and I'm not. I'll be there when she's at home, but when I have to be at the lab..."

Ben pulled his towel from around his neck and wiped his face above his beard before nodding. "I can do that. Recon's about all I'm good for right now, anyway." His golden eyes shifted to her, and Allie drifted back into the warmth of Gray's palm. "Let me know your work schedule. Unless I've got an appointment with one of my doctors or therapists, I'll be here."

Allie was torn between relief at knowing someone else would be watching her back, and concern that Gray had recruited her volatile patient to do the job. "You aren't going to hurt anyone, are you?"

A smile never cracked his face. Ben looked up at Gray, then over to the counter where Doug was writing on the calendar, then to her. "Do you need me to?"

"Um..."

"No." Gray chuckled despite her worry. "Right now, all I need is a point man to keep eyes on things here at the clinic. Report to me if anything looks hinky. More unwanted gifts arrive. Friesen not keeping his distance. Someone watching the building. Following Allie. That kind of thing."

"Yes, sir. I'll try not to let you down."

"Thank you, Sarge." Gray extended his right hand,

holding it without any sign of retreating for the several seconds it took the bearded veteran to respond to the friendly gesture.

Finally, Ben slapped his palm against Gray's and traded a sharp nod. Panic flared in his eyes when he realized Allie wanted to express her gratitude, as well. He held up both his hand and his hook, shook his head and stalked away toward the bank of lockers where patients stored their jackets and other personal items.

Allie hugged her arms around her waist. "He scares me sometimes."

"He's where I was when I first hit stateside with no legs, no job, just lost the woman I thought I was going to marry, with no more connection to the Corps and my buddies there. If Ben surrounds himself with the right people, finds a purpose outside of the military, he'll come around."

Allie glanced up at the man beside her. "Do you think he'll be okay?"

Green eyes met hers. "Do you think I'm okay?"

Allie summoned a weary smile. "You're okay enough for me. Thank you for coming. You being here this evening is exactly what I needed."

"I'm glad you texted me." That strand of hair had fallen over her cheek again and Gray sifted it between his thumb and finger before tucking it behind her ear one more time. "How much longer do you have to stay?"

"Ben and Ivy were my last patients of the day.

I need a few minutes to update my reports in their files."

"I'll pack my gear and grab my chair. Meet you out front."

Allie caught his arm when he turned toward the lockers. "Would you walk me out? I'll help with your chair, but I want to walk beside you." When she saw he was going to argue, she hastened to add, "I don't want the Mrs. Burroughses of the world to think that you're only my patient. Or neighbor. I want the world to know that I think you're hot, and that I'm laying claim to you. Maybe you're not ready for that. Maybe my timing sucks. I need the emotional support, a break from the endless stress. I want to hold your hand because I find comfort and strength in that. It's a mental thing—heaven knows I've had enough games played on me the past twenty-four hours—but—"

Gray shook his head. "As flattering as all that is, I'm not as mobile yet on foot. If something happens, my reaction time is slower than it is when I'm in the chair."

"If something happens, I'll take the guy out myself. At least stall him long enough until you can throw a punch or whack him over the head with a crutch."

He scrubbed his palm over his wheat-and-bronze stubble and muttered a curse. "I haven't thought about how'd I'd do hand-to-hand combat with the new me." He pulled his cell phone from his pocket. "I'd better talk to Aiden Murphy to see if he can give me a few tips. Or Chelsea's fiancé, Buck, runs security ops—"

"You do it the same way you did before, Marine. You're already in fighting shape. Assess the situation, look at the options available to you, rely on your training." She curled her fingers around his wrist to keep him from making the call. "Please. If your back is really bothering you and you need to use the chair, I understand. But I'm having a rare girlie moment here. I want to hold your hand, and I can't do that if one of us has to push you in your chair."

His eyes narrowed as he processed everything she'd just spewed out—from confessing she liked him to feeling beaten down by the relentless stress of reliving Noah's tortuous mind games to Gray remembering his military training. Then he dropped his gaze to his wrist and pulled back until he could capture her hand in his. "FYI? You're always girlie in my book." He squeezed before releasing her and glancing over at the counter. "Finish your paperwork. And steer clear of Friesen. I'll walk you out."

More to Read.
More to Love.

Get up to 4 Free Books – total value over $20.

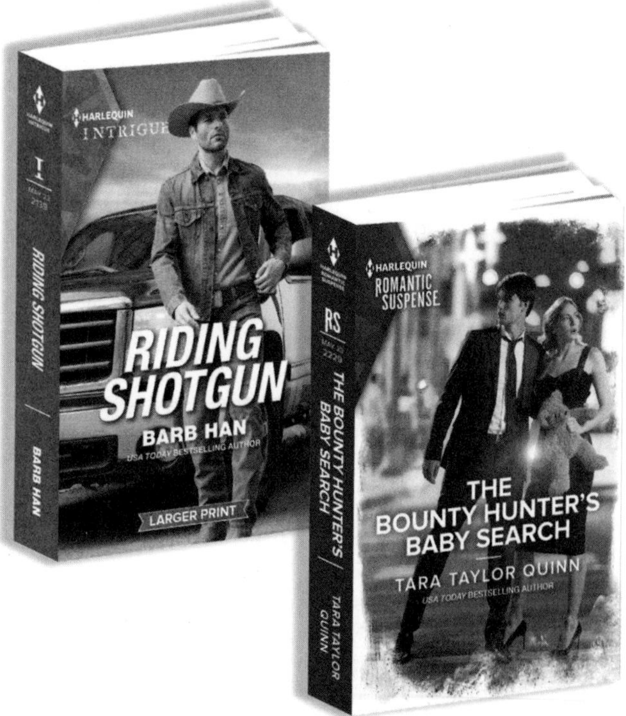

Don't miss out on the newest books from your favorite series!

See Inside for Details

Accepting your 2 free books and free gift (gift valued at approximately $10.00 retail) places you under no obligation to buy anything. You may keep the books and gift and return the shipping statement marked "cancel." If you do not cancel, approximately one month later we'll send you more books from the series you have chosen, and bill you at our low, subscribers-only discount price. Harlequin® Romantic Suspense books consist of 4 books each month and cost just $5.49 each in the U.S. or $6.24 each in Canada, a savings of at least 12% off the cover price. Harlequin Intrigue® Larger-Print books consist of 6 books each month and cost just $6.49 each in the U.S. or $6.99 each in Canada, a savings of at least 13% off the cover price. It's quite a bargain! Shipping and handling is just 50¢ per book in the U.S. and $1.25 per book in Canada*. You may return any shipment at our expense and cancel at any time by contacting customer service — or you may continue to receive monthly shipments at our low, subscribers-only discount price plus shipping and handling.

If offer card is missing write to: Harlequin Reader Service, P.O. Box 1341, Buffalo, NY 14240-8531 or visit www.ReaderService.com

BUSINESS REPLY MAIL

FIRST-CLASS MAIL PERMIT NO. 717 BUFFALO, NY

POSTAGE WILL BE PAID BY ADDRESSEE

HARLEQUIN READER SERVICE

PO BOX 1341

BUFFALO NY 14240-8571

NO POSTAGE NECESSARY IF MAILED IN THE UNITED STATES

Chapter Eight

By the time Allie got on to her computer tablet to update her patient files, Doug was thankfully gone. A quick scan of the PT room showed he must have left as soon as his shift ended. Maeve and a couple of the newer therapists had gotten stuck with the late shift and were busy with patients. But there was no sign of anyone who had caused her grief today.

There was no sign of Gray, either, but she assumed he'd be waiting for her in the lobby to walk her across the street to the staff parking garage. Thankfully, she'd found a spot on the ground floor, so he wouldn't have to negotiate the stairs or wrangle his chair onto the garage's small elevator. She figured she was already pushing him out of his comfort zone by insisting they walk. Add in her straightforward announcement that she thought he was hot, and she didn't want to press her luck and have him rebel and shut down on her the way he had last night at their building, before she'd discovered the break-in. She wanted that whole man-woman experience that she'd once hoped to have with Noah. After that relationship crashed and burned, no man had ever gotten under her skin and into her thoughts the way Grayson Malone did. She was ready to try being a couple again, ready to care, maybe even ready to give him her heart. She'd have to go slowly. The man was still working through some trust and self-esteem issues from the loss of his legs and his military career. But as long as he gave her a chance—gave them a chance—she would plant the seeds of a relationship and nurture it as much as he needed her to.

Or she'd go Navy lieutenant on his ass and shove him out of his comfort zone. She liked Gray. She wanted him. He challenged her intellectually and made her laugh. She trusted him enough to feel safe about lowering her guard. He wasn't put off by her strength, didn't try to diminish it the way Noah had. But he seemed to understand that just because she could handle almost anything on her own, she didn't always want to. She didn't have to wear herself out mentally and emotionally because when she needed a break, she believed Grayson Malone would have her six.

After double-checking tomorrow's schedule against her phone and the written calendar to ensure there were no more discrepancies, Allie closed down her computer. She waved good night to Maeve, then opened her locker in the back room and put the tablet away. She slipped the long strap of her envelope purse over her shoulder and pulled out her keys with the attached pepper spray canister, sliding them into the pocket of her scrub pants. She closed her locker, spun the combination lock, then hurried out through the lobby to meet Gray at the exit. He had his wheelchair folded beside him, his equipment bag slung over his right shoulder, and he was tall and handsome and perfect for her.

Well, almost perfect. She noticed he had one crutch cuffed around his right forearm. Better than two crutches, but she had to ask, "Do you really need that?"

He held the crutch up and swished it back and forth as if he was wielding some sort of samurai sword. "In case I have to whack somebody over the head."

Allie laughed out loud. "You really did listen to that whole spiel I gave."

"I listen when you talk, Lieutenant. Then I process the words and the meaning behind them until I reach the logical conclusion."

She loved it when he talked all sciencey geek to her. "And what conclusion did you reach?"

"That I want to hold hands with you, too." Gray held his left hand out to her. "Shall we?" When she took it, he sealed her hand in his strong, gentle grip.

She pushed the automatic button to open the door and was greeted by the rumbling of thunder in the distance. Allie tipped her face to the dark gray clouds gathering overhead. The air already smelled like ozone ahead of the cold front. “Looks like rain. Do you want me to run and get the car and pick you up over here?”

“It’s not raining yet. And you’re not going into a shadowy parking garage on your own.” He tugged on her hand, and she fell easily into step beside him. “You said we were walking. Let’s walk.”

The first drops hit before they reached the entrance to the garage. Allie dashed ahead, pushing the folded wheelchair out of the rain. When she turned back to help Gray, he was already moving at what looked like a three-legged trot. Although it was only a matter of seconds before they hurried beneath the protective overhang, the clouds skipped the sprinkling stage and opened up with a steady downpour. It was enough to soak the shoulders of her jacket and drip through her hair until it trickled along her scalp. Once they got inside, Gray released her to scrub his hand over the top of his short hair and shake off a palmful of water.

“Well, that was exciting.” Allie plucked her scrubs away from her shoulders and breasts, then shook at the sudden drop in temperature against her wet skin. “I’m not far from here. Next aisle over, about halfway down.”

“Wait.” He propped his crutch against his thigh and shrugged out of his hoodie. He flung it around her shoulder and urged her to poke her arms into the sleeves. "You're shivering."

"You're wet, too." She half-heartedly protested the gallant gesture, already absorbing the lingering warmth from his body and dipping her nose to inhale his scent clinging to the cotton.

"My bag kept it pretty dry. And I like you wearing my jacket. The gray brings out the soft color of your eyes." Before she could savor the compliment, he zipped the hoodie all the way to the top, then pulled the neckline together beneath her chin before resting his forehead against hers. "Besides, you've got that freaky cold-natured thing going on and I need to warm you up. I'm not holding on to ice cube hands."

Allie burst out with a laugh and was rewarded with a smile. Gray swung his bag over the shoulder of his T-shirt, hooked the crutch over his forearm and reached for her hand. As they walked farther into the parking garage, the pungent fumes of gasoline and oil spills on the concrete gradually overpowered the fresh scent of the rain. And even though he was walking beside her as she'd requested, her hand folded snugly into his, she couldn't help but notice the hyper alertness of his gaze, scanning each and every car they passed. He walked with his typical uneven gait, but his broad shoulders were back, his balance squared exactly as she had taught him over his hips. The man was charming and considerate, and completely on guard against any unseen threat.

His watchfulness had Allie scanning up and down the long aisle of vehicles, too. "Are you sure we can trust Ben with a security detail?"

"I think he's looking for something to focus on. Keeping watch would have been drilled into him by the Army. The setting and the enemy might be different, but the job should feel familiar."

She wondered if being on guard like this was familiar to him, too. And if that was a good thing, or a job that made him doubt his current abilities even more. "You're sure you're not trusting him just because he's military? After all, Noah was military, too. The government wouldn't need a prison the size of NAVCONBRIG CHASN if every soldier and sailor was a saint."

Gray stopped and swung his gaze around as if he'd heard a noise she had missed. She saw nothing but rain falling in a dreary gray curtain beyond the entrance. That must have been all he could make out, too, because he tugged her into step beside him again. "You think Ben could be doing this to you?"

"He seems too hotheaded to do the research to recreate incidents that happened before. And I never met him until he came to the clinic as a patient a few weeks ago. But he does seem to have a pretty wide angry streak running through him."

"I'll keep him on my suspect list. One of the reasons I agreed to his help is so we can keep a closer eye on *him*. A lot of times, a perp will insert himself into an investigation to keep tabs on it and get an extra thrill of seeing the aftermath of his handiwork."

"Like me freaking out at work?"

"If that was you freaking out, I'm not worried. Once you had a chance to clear your head, you took charge of the situation. Everyone got what they needed, and you came out of it looking like a champ."

"Which would have totally pissed off Noah." Allie had to release Gray's hand to pull out her keys as they neared her car. "And you're convinced someone besides him is behind this?"

"I think it's a possibility. I don't want KCPD or the crime lab to focus solely on your ex and miss a threat that's closer to home. Someone like Ben, who seems a little unstable, or Friesen, who wants to get in your pants. Have you talked about what you went through in Jacksonville to anyone at work?"

Allie shrugged as she hit the remote and the trunk popped open. "Maeve, a little bit. I told her I had a bad breakup. I didn't tell her about him sabotaging my car and running me off the road. She said she's familiar with lousy exes—we commiserated."

"Friesen could have overheard, done a little research. Maybe he's punishing you for turning him down—or maybe he expects you to turn to him for comfort."

"That'll never happen." Allie frowned as another possible suspect sprang to mind. "Bubba hits on me when I run into him in the building. I try not to be home when he's doing repairs. He's been in my apartment twice in the past month. First to repair my garbage disposal, then to replace it."

"Bubba Summerfield? Our building super?" Gray shook his head. "I didn't get an upgrade. I'll make a note to double-check whose apartments he's been going into recently, and how often. If you've been singled out, I'll have Officer Cutler question him again."

"While Doug is annoying, Bubba feels harmless. To be honest, I can't see him having the brains or the patience to stalk me without revealing his identity. He'd brag on purpose or let something slip."

Allie reached for the wheelchair, but Gray was already lifting it and loading it into the trunk. "Unless someone is telling him what to do. We're still combing through the visitor log at NAVCONBRIG CHASN. Someone in your world here in KC may have a connection to Boggs."

She stepped back as he loaded the bag, as well. "This feels like before. Booking the two most vocal, least flexible patients who'll raise the biggest stink at the same time? I wouldn't give myself a headache like that. And the anonymous flowers are just like Jacksonville. Things seem normal on the surface. If you're outside looking in, nothing seems wrong." She hugged her arms around her waist, standing back as he retrieved the second metal crutch. "But I know things are off. There's someone out there, plotting against me—undermining me, isolating me, forcing me to relive the worst time of my life. It's all leading to whatever *Payback* means. I don't think I can go through this again."

Gray closed the trunk and turned to her. "Look at me. You're the strongest woman I've ever met. And I know a few."

"I don't feel strong. A little mix-up like double-booking patients shouldn't have rattled me like that. Then the flowers came, and Doug was being too *helpful*, and I lost it." She reached up and touched her fingertips to the corner of his mouth. "I'm sorry if I made you feel uncomfortable with that kiss. I know you're super conscious of how people perceive you when you're in your chair. The last thing I want to do is screw up anything between us. I mean, I want there to be something between us. But I know this is going to get worse before it gets better, and you're not going to want to be a part of that."

"Come here." Gray shifted both crutches to one hand and tunneled the fingers of his free hand into the base of her ponytail.

Not the reaction she'd been expecting. She thought he'd have a logical argument, a sympathetic word. Instead, he palmed the side of her neck and pulled her into his kiss.

Gray's mouth covered hers in a thorough stamp of possession. There was no hesitation, no getting acquainted, no apology. His lips moved against hers, stroking, taking, claiming. His tongue teased the seam of her lips and she willingly opened for him. Allie felt him rocking closer as he slid his tongue inside her mouth to dance with hers. Allie's hands fisted in the front of his T-shirt, then slid up around his neck to palm the prickly crispness of his damp hair. Moving her fingers across the fine shape of his head stirred up the scents of rain and man, until she was surrounded by it, consumed by the smells she craved so much.

It was as if they'd kissed a hundred times before. Gray's mouth felt familiar on hers. His stubble teased her sensitive skin and his firm lips and raspy tongue soothed. It was just his mouth on hers, his hand in her hair, the tips of her breasts pearling and rubbing against his chest. The kiss was commanding, seductive, a testament to his strength and control. Gray's lips claiming hers blotted out all thoughts except the rightness of the two of them together. Two wounded warriors. Two kindred spirits. Man. Woman. Comfort. Need.

And then Gray pulled his mouth from hers with a deep-pitched groan. His fingertips were still tangled in her hair, pulsing at the nape of her neck. He dropped his forehead to rest against hers, his breath gusting against her face. "Damn, woman. Shouldn't have kissed you like that."

Allie was feeling a little like she'd just pushed herself to run a six-minute mile, riding an endorphin high, gasping for air and equilibrium. She clung to Gray's shoulders because they were the most solid thing she could anchor herself to at the moment. She looked up into his turbulent green eyes. "Why did you?"

"I needed to distract you—break the downward spiral of those thoughts."

Her nostrils flared as she took in a deep breath and tried to hide her disappointment. She dropped her hands to the slightly more neutral location of his biceps and pulled her forehead from his. "You kissed me to distract me?" Her voice was still husky with passion, and she tried to tease. "Smooth, Malone. Your dating skills are a little rusty."

He tangled more of her ponytail between his fingers and tightened his grip on her neck, silently asking her not to retreat. "For the record, your kissing me at the clinic didn't make me uncomfortable. What made me uncomfortable was how badly I wanted to take you in my arms and turn that kiss into something more." His gaze dropped to her mouth. "I wanted to kiss you. I wanted visceral proof that we share a connection. That we're a team." His eyes found hers again. "I swear you will not be alone this time. I'm not going to abandon you to some superior officer who controls your fate. I'm not sure I can hold up my end of the deal, but I want to try. My brain says help you, protect you, kiss you. My body doesn't always comply with what my instincts and training tell it to do. But I wanted to try. I wanted to comfort you. I wanted to find out what your lips tasted like." He pressed the pad of his thumb to her swollen bottom lip and nerve endings tingled in her breasts and between her thighs. "A perfect blend of sweetness and sass, by the way."

This man. How could he ever think he was anything less than a potent, virile male? "Wow. That's a much better explanation why you wanted to kiss me."

He chuckled deep in his throat, a gravelly, sexy sound. "I'm working on my flirting skills. My therapist said I needed to up my game."

"I'll make a note of the improvements in your file."

He replaced his thumb with a quick brush of his lips over hers. "Are we really doing this? Are we falling for each other?"

"I'm already halfway there. The heart and hormones are willing. Not too sure about the timing, though."

He nodded. "We're both practical people. We've both been burned pretty badly by past relationships. We both have complications in our lives."

She couldn't argue with any of that. She could do slow if that was what he needed. Or she could throw caution to the wind and jump in with both feet. She had a feeling Gray wasn't sure how he wanted to move forward yet. But they were moving forward. They were on the same page now about the possibility of a relationship, and that gave her hope. Allie hadn't felt hope for a very long time. "I'm glad to have the Marines on my side. The crime lab. You."

He finally pulled away entirely to slide the cuff of his crutch on to his left forearm. "Let my team do their job. We'll find answers, confirm the who, and figure out the how and why. In the meantime, you're staying with me. You're wearing my hoodie. And you're never alone, not until we catch whoever is behind this."

"That was an awfully bossy set of rules, Malone. It chafes against my independent nature." He started to explain his reasoning, but she cut him off. "But it makes me feel better—it makes me feel safer—to share this psychological terror campaign with someone. However, I have a few rules I'm laying down, too. One, I want you to kiss me like that again. Maybe several times. And two…" She reached for his hand and laced their fingers together. "I want to sit on your lap and bury my nose against that sexy, manly scent that comes off your skin while you hold me in your arms. Tight. I want to cuddle."

His cheekbones turned rosy with a blush. "That's it? Those are your rules?"

"And I want to share expenses and help take care of your apartment. Also, I missed my run today, so I'll want to exercise tomorrow. It's the best stress reducer for me—plus, I want to stay in fighting shape in case I need to, you know, fight. And if you and your friends are coming over Saturday afternoon to help clean my apartment, I insist on buying beer or sodas and pizza for everyone."

"This is getting to be a long list. Anything else?"

"Maybe." She tilted her chin and leaned in to kiss the corner of his mouth. "But I don't want to scare you off."

"You haven't yet, Tate."

The rumblings of thunder and steady drumbeat of rain against the pavement must have masked the sound of an engine starting. But there was no mistaking the squeal of tires fighting for traction as a car rounded the end of the aisle and raced toward them. "Gray?"

For a split second she flashed back to the sounds of Noah's truck racing up in her rearview mirror, ramming her car and spinning her over the railing of the bridge. Her breath lodged in her chest, and she couldn't seem to move. The bright beam of headlights blinded her.

"Allie!"

A vise clamped around her waist and she was off her feet, flying backward, out of the path of the car bearing down on her. In a span of milliseconds, she realized the lights kept her from seeing the driver's face. She felt the breeze of the car rushing past. Gray lost his footing and they were falling until he caught her bumper with one strong arm and pushed them both upright.

A fist-sized projectile flew out the open, passenger-side window and Gray shouted a warning, even as she tried to push him out of the way. “Look out!”

A glass jar sailed through the air and shattered against the trunk of Allie’s car. She felt a sharp nick on her cheek and something warm and viscous oozing down her face and neck. The car careened around the corner and left the garage with a cacophony of honking horns as it skidded into traffic.

Gray’s arm was still anchored around her waist as he righted himself over his legs and pulled out his cell phone.

“Are you all right?” Allie asked, wondering at the breathless, distant sound of her voice. Spots of red dotted the sleeve of his T-shirt and bare arm. “What the hell?”

Gray dropped his crutches to free his hands. He put the phone to his ear and touched his fingers to her jawline. “Is any of that yours?”

“Is any of what mine?”

“The blood.” He studied her with unblinking intensity as his call picked up. “This is Grayson Malone. KCPD Crime Lab. Someone just tried to kill my girlfriend and me. Attempted hit-and-run. The car’s gone. No license plate. Send units. Send a bus. Send Lexi Callahan-Murphy and her team from the lab.” After giving their location, he hung up. “Talk to me.”

Allie touched the cut on her cheek and dragged her fingers through the ooze, trying to shake off the shock and the memories and understand what had happened. Her hand came away covered with blood. The hoodie she loved so much had rivulets of scarlet goo running down the front. "I think it's just a little cut on my cheek. Where is this all coming from?" There was blood pooling on the trunk of her car, running over the edge and dripping off the bumper. Shards of glass littered the pavement at her feet. When she reached for a curved piece of glass on her trunk, Gray caught her wrist and pulled her away from the car. "He threw a jar of blood at us? What does that mean? Gray?"

"I'm right here with you, babe. Don't touch anything else." He brushed aside a lock of hair that clung to her cheek and tucked it behind her ear. "I want nothing more than to take you in my arms right now and hold you tight."

"Yes. That's what I want, too." She stepped toward him, but his grip on her wrist and cheek tightened, strong-arming her out of his personal space. The mix of anguish and anger on his face made her retreat another half a step. "What is it?"

The shock dissipated with a frightening realization.

"You can't hold me."

He shook his head. "I'm sorry, babe. You're the crime scene."

Chapter Nine

Gray opened his eyes to the golden-orange glow of sunrise bleeding into the apartment around the blinds at the living room window. His bed was hard, and so was he. His mind snapped awake at the unfamiliar sensations, and he quickly processed each one.

Not in his bed.

Not alone.

For a split second, the urge to escape to familiar territory jolted through him. But a long strand of honey-blond hair caught in the scruff of his beard and stirred up the scents of a faint flowery shampoo. Allie.

He breathed her in again and felt his body relax. He grinned. Well, most of his body. That seemed to be happening a lot when he spent time with Allie.

Waking up curled around a woman's body was an experience he'd forgotten—her back to his chest, her bottom nestled against his groin, his thighs tucked behind hers, and nothing more. After Brittany's teary-eyed freak-out about missing half his legs, he'd expected that every woman would be hesitant to be physically intimate with him.

But not Allie Tate. In fact, she seemed to seek him out—to hold his hand, to snuggle against his arm on the couch while they talked through the events of the afternoon and evening. Although the hoodie he'd given her yesterday had been bagged up and taken to the crime lab to process the blood sample on it, she had longingly eyed the one he'd put on—the gray-and-red one with *Marines* written on it. He'd happily handed it over for her to wear like a robe over the T-shirt and lounge pants she'd changed into after cleaning up. There was something possessively right about a special woman wearing *his* clothes—even if it was an oversize, well-worn sweatshirt with a faded logo on the chest. He felt protective, and more like a man than he had since that RPG had blown up his convoy.

Even when he'd been 100 percent before that last deployment, Brittany hadn't been this much of a toucher. Yeah, they'd had sex. They'd hugged and kissed. But it had never been like this—like something would sneak in and tear her apart if she didn't have contact with him. Even in sleep, Allie clung to the forearm he'd cinched around her waist.

Last night, it was clear she was too wired to sleep. So, he'd streamed a movie for them. But she wasn't really watching it. They'd discussed Noah Boggs and how the progression of events here in KC echoed the mind games he'd used to intimidate and isolate her back in Jacksonville. They were both exhausted, but rehashing the clues and possibilities wasn't helping her relax. So, Gray had put some soft music on and offered to hold her until she got sleepy, with the promise he'd tuck her in and let her sleep in as long as she needed in the morning.

The strain beside Allie's gray-blue eyes had softened. She'd tucked her hands beneath his left arm, curled her knees up over his thigh and rested her cheek against his shoulder. Then she'd made a sweet joke about how her feet were as cold as her hands, so, in a way, he was lucky he didn't have anything below his knees she could press them against. He felt her hold her breath for a few seconds, anxious to learn if she'd offended him or amused him with her practicality. Allie Tate talked to him as if he was a normal man—she prodded and teased, argued and laughed. She didn't make a big deal about his disability, but she never turned her head and shied away from it, either.

So, Gray had laughed at his good fortune, rolled her onto her back and proceeded to kiss her the way she said she liked, the way he liked, with grabby hands and dueling tongues and sexy moans, with those sweet, small breasts tightening up like buttons and rubbing against his chest—until she'd yawned against his mouth. Gray wasn't offended. Instead, he was pleased that he had a way to distract her from the thoughts that plagued her. Her day had been hellishly long and full of stress and she needed her rest. Besides, when he lay down behind her and she cuddled into him, Gray felt a sense of rightness, of hope, swelling inside his chest.

Maybe he'd been falling in love with his neighbor a little bit more each day over the past few months they'd lived side by side and worked together at the clinic. But he hadn't let himself act on those feelings. He'd been guarding his heart with an emotional flak vest, afraid of not being enough, of not being the man a woman needed.

But bloody messages, frightening mind games and someone with a devious, dangerous plan forcing himself into Allie's life had pierced that vest and forced the man inside him to shove aside the bad memories and self-doubts. That car racing toward them tonight could have shattered every bone in Allie's body. She'd been in shock, on the verge of some kind of flashback, and wasn't moving. If his reaction time had been any slower, she would have ended up with a lot worse than a cut on her cheek. He could have lost her before they ever had a real chance to begin. The woman sleeping so trustingly in his arms this morning was a gift he would protect with his life. He wanted her. He needed her to be safe.

But caring like this might get him hurt again. Allie was a strong woman with an independent spirit. Noah Boggs had tried to frighten that out of her, and he hadn't succeeded. She'd learned how to endure all on her own. Without a man. Without anyone. Maybe once he found answers and the man terrorizing her was behind bars, she wouldn't need him anymore. She'd see him for what he really was—a has-been not good for much beyond running scientific tests and keeping her warm—and go back to being alone. If he couldn't have a real relationship with Allie, Gray didn't want any. He could distance himself as her neighbor—be friendly and polite but limit the chances of running into her by changing his schedule. He'd probably have to find a new physical therapist, though. He wasn't sure he could deal with her touching him and it not meaning anything.

And if he failed to keep her alive and safe, Gray wasn't sure he could come back from that. It would be proof that he wasn't the man he used to be—that he'd never be that Marine again. If he felt guilty about surviving a war zone when his buddies had died, the guilt he'd feel at losing this good woman would break him.

Allie whimpered in her sleep and hugged herself more tightly around his forearm, clearly agitated by some subconscious thought. He kissed the back of her neck and shushed her back into a deeper slumber. She sighed in contentment and whispered his name in her sleep.

Ah, hell. He was in so much trouble. He was in love with her.

That flak vest he'd put up around his emotions was useless now. If he wanted Allie—if he wanted to earn her love, in return—he'd need to move past all his personal baggage and fight for her, show her he was the man she could love and depend on. He'd trained his body as a Marine. He'd trained his mind as a criminalist. He needed to train his heart to be the man Allie Tate could love.

Baby steps, Malone. He masked a chuckle at the irony of that statement.

First, he needed to extricate himself from Allie's grasp and dress and get ready for the day—a task he still wasn't sure he wanted the woman he needed to impress to witness. Pushing himself up, then pulling himself along the back of the couch until he could move freely, Gray spider-walked to the end of the sectional where he'd removed his prostheses and pads last night. There was no point in putting them on until he got through his shower. His wheelchair was still beside the front door where they'd left it to dry after getting rained on. There was no way to do this gracefully.

He glanced back at Allie, tucked the comforter around her sleeping form. Then, dragging his legs and crutches behind him, he scuttled into the bedroom and adjoining master bath.

ALLIE WASN'T SURE why Gray was so quiet this morning. Snugged up against the furnace of his body, she'd gotten the best night's sleep she'd had in months. She had a feeling the night could have ended with something more, based on her body's wicked reaction to his kisses and his obvious response to hers. Even though giving herself to Gray was on her future agenda, he'd been smart enough to see her fatigue and had ended the make-out session on the couch with the promise of holding her through the night.

Maybe he was disappointed they hadn't gone all the way? Maybe he was still hung up on her perception of his physical attractiveness and ultimate reliability, and he'd been relieved she'd been willing to stop. Maybe he wasn't a cuddler, and her clinginess had been a turn-off—although the man sure was a pro at it.

He was all ready for the day by the time she'd roused herself from sleep and gone into the guest bathroom to freshen up. He'd cooked them a healthy breakfast of veggie omelets and toast while she packed a bag of clothes she could change into at work. He'd encouraged her to go down to the building's gym and run on the treadmill for about twenty minutes until they had to leave for the clinic. While she insisted that getting back to her running schedule would be good for both her physical and mental health, Gray was adamant that she not run outside by herself. Either she needed a running buddy, or she was doing it here in the building. After the events of the past few days, Allie hadn't argued—she had no desire to be out there in the world alone with an enemy lurking in the unseen corners of her life.

She was pleased to see that he'd put on his prosthetic legs again after getting out of the shower. Legs or chair or neither, Grayson Malone was a hottie who had awakened both her heart and her hormones. But the therapist in her knew he needed to spend more time getting used to his new prostheses. He probably worried that they wouldn't fit properly and would start rubbing and causing lesions like the last pair. But that had been his own fault for working out to the extreme and negating the original fit. He needed to learn to be comfortable in any situation and feel confident that he was in control of his body—not that his chair or prostheses controlled him.

She was also glad they'd already made arrangements for him to drive them to work today. That way she didn't miss her car quite so much while it was impounded at the lab and then sent on to her dealer's repair center to get detailed and have the dent removed from where the blood-filled jar had hit.

Conversation over breakfast was polite, but nothing too deep or personal. They'd probably covered way too much of that the past two nights on his sofa. She wondered if he was thinking about the investigation, or if he was regretting that he'd gotten involved with her mess of a life, or if he was simply a quiet guy in the morning.

When she asked him about it, he tapped his watch and pointed out the time, reminding her that she needed to get going if she wanted any time in the gym downstairs, or they'd both be late for work.

Allie crossed to his side of the table and folded her arms in front of her. "Changing the subject is not an answer to my question, Malone."

He chuckled before pushing back his chair and standing up. A ripple of awareness shivered through her as he straightened above her. Mistaking her tremors for her susceptibility to cold temps, he cupped her shoulders and ran his hands up and down her arms. "Keep the jacket."

"Still not an answer to the question. But thank you." She was reassured that he was touching her again. She returned the favor and splayed her hand against his chest. "Do I need to be worried about anything?"

"No. Nothing new." He leaned in to press a quick kiss to her lips before pulling away. "I've got a lot on my mind this morning—some things I need to figure out. I don't like feeling that this guy is smarter than I am. I promised you answers. I haven't got any yet."

"You will." Allie gathered up their plates and rinsed them in the kitchen sink. "And last night? Are you okay with the way things turned out?"

"I haven't been in a relationship since Brittany, so I feel a little rusty. But I'm very okay. I figure if the time is right, it will feel right. For both of us." He brought the pan and spatula to the sink and stood beside her. "You?"

"I'm better now that you're talking to me again."

"I'll finish these." Gray nudged her aside with his shoulder. "Go. Run. I'll be down in twenty, twenty-five minutes. Do not go outside."

"Yes, sir." Allie saluted him, then tilted her lips up to kiss his stubbled jaw.

With the promise that he'd get her bag and purse loaded into his van, Allie grabbed her keys and hurried out the door.

Fifteen minutes later, Allie was rethinking her effort to clear her head.

Stretching her muscles, expanding her lungs and raising her heart rate felt good. But there was an unspoken rule that runners enjoyed their alone time. She was here to get her endorphins sparking and find that zen sense of peace in her mind.

But even the whirring of the treadmill and the rhythmic stamp of her feet couldn't drown out Bubba Summerfield's meaningless prattle. The short and stocky building super had spent the last ten minutes up on an aluminum ladder, changing the fluorescent lightbulbs in the ceiling. A friendly greeting and going about his business in the same room was one thing, but she'd already learned that Mrs. Wyatt who lived across the hall from her had complained about the noise from the crime lab team and curiosity seekers who'd been at her apartment the other night. And she'd been terrified to have Aiden Murphy's K-9 partner, Blue, in the building, even though the dog had been well-behaved and had only growled at Bubba himself for barging in. Bubba had laughed off that part of his story, saying he had never been very good with dogs, anyway, that he was more of a cat person.

Allie adjusted the incline of the treadmill and quickened her pace, mentally trying to outrun the man. She thought the rattle of him moving the ladder behind her was a sign he was leaving, but he set it up right next to the treadmill and climbed up. And kept talking. Allie tried to blank the tan coveralls from her peripheral vision, and picture images of Grayson Malone kissing her like she'd never been kissed before, popping the suction off his prosthetic legs last night and allowing her to massage some lotion into the scarred stumps of his thighs—which she suspected had been the epitome of trust for him, making the contact feel like a secret intimacy between lovers. She remembered how he had wrapped his body around hers in a way that chased away every troubling thought and potential nightmare and allowed her to sleep.

But Bubba's fingers wrapped around the handle of the treadmill for balance as he descended the ladder, and she nearly stumbled as she shied away from the almost touch. Why hadn't she thought to bring her earbuds and a podcast to listen to?

"...the family in 4B. Since they didn't pay the pet deposit for that cat, replacing the carpet will be coming out of their pocketbook." He moved the ladder to the last ceiling light, thankfully beyond arm's reach. Apparently, he didn't need a comment to continue the conversation. "You know, that carpet won't be in for a couple of days. I've got time this afternoon and tomorrow to get into your apartment and start bleaching walls and repainting them. Not sure what I'm going to do about your cabinets, though. If I can't get them clean with some good elbow grease, I might have to replace them."

"No." Allie's ponytail caught in her mouth as she turned to Bubba. She pulled the strands from her lips and faced forward again. "I've got friends coming Saturday afternoon to help with the cleanup." At least, Gray had promised *his* friends from the crime lab would come. Her rhythm had gotten a little off, so she pushed the button to slow her pace. "I don't want anyone in my apartment." She wasn't about to explain the sense of violation she still felt about the break-in, the loss of control that she wasn't calling the shots in her own life anymore. The chatty super didn't need to know any of that. "Thanks, anyway, though," she added, hoping to end the conversation, and run that last couple of minutes in peace and quiet.

"What difference does it make?" Was that a snap of frustration in his tone? "You haven't been staying there, anyway. Isn't my work good enough?"

"You've been watching my apartment?" Allie dropped the incline of her run and slowed her pace to a cool-down speed.

"Hey, I'm part of the security around this building. It's my job to keep an eye on things."

"It's not your job to know my personal business."

"It's no secret around here that you and Mr. Malone are sweet on each other. You two doing the nasty yet?"

"What?" She tried to make eye contact with him, but Bubba was too far behind her, and she couldn't risk tripping and falling. "Who are you going to share that tidbit of gossip with?"

"I don't have to share it." He snickered as if he couldn't understand why she'd be offended by his question. "Everybody knows stuff in this building. I'm not the only one watching you guys."

"Who else is watching me?" Allie pulled the safety key from the treadmill keyboard, stopping it abruptly the same time she heard Grayson's voice from the doorway.

"Get your eyes off her ass, Summerfield." Now, *that* was the voice of a Marine.

With her equilibrium still spinning a bit after the abrupt stop to her run, she reached for Gray's hand where he clasped his crutch. He instantly released the handle and turned his hand to hold on to her, instead. "You don't speak to Lieutenant Tate like that, either. What goes on inside any apartment in this building is none of your business."

"Easy, Mr. Malone. I didn't mean nothing about the two of you hooking up." The super put his hands up in a gesture of placating surrender. "But it's true?

The two of you are together? I didn't want to believe what folks were saying."

"What folks? Who's talking about us?" Allie demanded.

"I kind of fancied asking you out myself."

Allie glared into his beady brown eyes and wondered what he found so amusing about this conversation. But she spoke to Gray. "Bubba said he's not the only person who's been watching me."

"I need names, Summerfield. A description. Who have you seen?"

Grayson's glare must have been a little more intimidating because Bubba retreated half a step. His keys rattled as he rested his forearms against his tool belt. "Some guy. I've seen him in the garage or parked out front or across the street. Because, you know, your apartment is in the front of the building."

"Some guy?" Gray demanded clarification while Allie's spirit withered a little at the thought of spies all around her, and she'd been completely unaware. God, hadn't she learned anything from Noah? How had she gotten so complacent? "I need more."

Bubba shrugged. "I can't tell you much. It's not like I've seen his face. He's always hiding it. In the shadows or with a hat. But I know he doesn't live here."

"How do you know that?" Gray pushed.

"Doesn't have a building permit sticker on his windshield."

"Can you describe the car?" Allie asked, dredging up a vision of headlights racing toward her, and a blur of black flying past.

Bubba grinned, looking much happier to be talking to her than to Gray. "An older car. Four doors. Black. And no, I didn't get a license number."

Gray reached into his back pocket to pull out his wallet and a business card. He handed his contact information at the crime lab over to the super. "You see that guy or the car again, call me."

Bubba tucked the card into his coveralls. "Okay."

"I mean it. It's a matter of personal security for Lieutenant Tate."

Bubba frowned. "Allie? This guy wasn't watching her."

"You just said—"

"Mr. Malone. I think he's watching *you*."

Chapter Ten

Cutting the corner into the crime lab parking lot too close and bumping his tire over the curb was the least of Gray's problems today. True, he wouldn't be driving his van in the Indy 500 anytime soon, or running any races on his prosthetic legs, or winning any bachelor-of-the-month contests. But he damn well thought he'd been on the trail of the right stalker, at least. Now he wasn't so sure.

Somehow, a discussion of Chelsea O'Brien's wedding plans had led to the women of the KCPD crime lab meeting in Lexi Callahan-Murphy's office over lunch, while Gray and the men he worked with sat around a big table in the lab's memorial lounge, polishing off sandwiches and takeout, and drinking bottles of water and cups of coffee.

"Sorry you all got roped into Chelsea's plans for the wedding." Buck Buckner, Chelsea's fiancé, was a veteran cop with a bulldog face, salt-and-pepper hair, and an absolute soft spot for the lab's quirky computer guru. "But since she grew up without a family and never had so much as a birthday party, much less a fancy dress-up event like a wedding, I want her to have whatever she wants."

"We get that, man." Rufus King, Buck's former partner at KCPD, and now the uniformed ops sergeant who helped the director run the crime lab, rubbed his palm over his shaved head. "Chelsea's part of our family here at the lab now. We want to help the two of you celebrate. Besides, we are all behind her getting your grumpy butt married off and out of our hair." He tapped his mahogany scalp. "So to speak."

There was shared laughter among friends, some congratulatory comments about the marriage, teasing about the improvement in Buck's personality since meeting Chelsea, along with the absence of Rufus's hair. But they were guys, and that was about all the talk about weddings and romance they could manage. Conversations around the table quickly turned back to work, as these informal bull sessions in the lounge usually did.

Gray sat at one end of the long table, his crutches leaning against the table beside him as he swirled tepid coffee around in his travel mug. "It's not lost on me that I'm the lab's blood expert, and there's an unnatural amount of blood involved in Allie's case." Not for the first time that morning, he wondered why he hadn't made the connection sooner. Or maybe there was no connection, and he was trying to force the coincidences of bloody warnings into the answers he so desperately wanted. "If this perp is tailing me, maybe it's just a means to get to Allie. I'm not the one this guy is trying to gaslight. She's the one who's gotten hurt."

"The super could be an idiot," Shane suggested, taking a bite of a sprinkle-laden cookie that had probably been decorated by his toddler son. "You and Allie live next door to each other, so you're bound to run into each other a lot. Plus, you commute every day you have PT in the morning. Not to mention all the time you've spent at the clinic. If you guys are together, who can say if they're watching her or you?"

"You think there's a connection?" Mac Taylor, the director of the crime lab, sat at the opposite end of the table. If possible, his brain operated with even more pure logic than Gray's did. "Between Allie being stalked and the presence of so much blood?"

Gray leaned back in his chair. "Well, I don't believe in cosmic karma. Why not use paint in her apartment? Why not toss corrosive liquid that could do real damage to her or her car? Why real blood on that florist's card? Why throw a jar of it at her?"

Brian Stockman, the oldest uniformed officer in the room, who oversaw the CSIU, or Crime Scene Investigation Unit, and coordinated their crime scene assignments with the police department, said, "Technically, the driver targeted both of you, tried to run you both down."

Gray scrubbed at the stubble of his beard. "Maybe I've been looking at this all wrong. Focusing on Allie. Maybe this is about hurting *me*. We're not a couple, not until recent events threw us together. She might be collateral damage."

Aiden Murphy snorted a laugh. He leaned against the beverage counter where his K-9 partner, Blue, was dozing at his feet. "Are you kidding? You two have been shootin' sparks off each other for weeks now. She always makes a point of coming over to talk to you at the clinic, even when you're not assigned to her. You do that dancing thing."

"Dancing thing?"

"I've seen it, too," Shane pointed out.

"Yeah, I don't know what kind of therapy holding on to each other like that's supposed to be—" Aiden went on.

"It's to work on my balance—"

"—but every time I've given you a ride, you two always seem to be touching each other. Lexi's commented on it, too." As usual, Aiden smiled at the mention of his wife. "I can't tell you how many times she's asked me if you two are dating. I think she wanted to set you up with a friend if you were free."

Gray frowned. "She doesn't need to set me up with anybody. I'm not interested."

Except for a couple of snickers, the silence around the table told Gray that he had just made Aiden's point.

"Allie and I look like a couple?"

As usual, his buddy Jackson waited until he had something important to say before speaking. "Drop everything here and get you to the clinic when she sends you an SOS?"

While part of his brain was processing the idea that others had seen him and Allie together as a couple before he'd even considered the possibility, Gray was figuring out something quite different. "Anyone watching me would mistake us for a couple, too." Jackson's reminder of his response to Allie's text for help finally convinced him. "If they wanted to hurt me—not physically hurt me, but tear me up inside, distract me, get me off my game—they'd go after Allie."

Even though he ran his own security firm now, Buck still thought like a cop. "But why replay the scenario of all the things her ex did to her? Not wishing anyone to put his hands on her the way they did Chels, but why not just attack her? Why the mind games?"

Gray knew the answer to that. "Because that's how you hurt her the most. Allie's a tough, confident woman. Trained in the military. A strong runner." He thumped his chest, fully admitting his guilt. "Doesn't put up with guff from stubborn patients or creepy coworkers. She'd be hard to take down physically. But you get into her head, and it makes her question her surroundings and doubt herself. Takes her back to the scariest, loneliest time of her life."

Buck seemed to understand. "Whether it's physical or psychological, someone threatens the woman you love, and that's all you can think about."

Love? Yeah, these guys had read his feelings for Allie long before he'd admitted them to himself.

Aiden moved up to the table. "The need to watch over your woman makes a heck of a diversion, too. You got any big cases you've been neglecting?"

Rufus King was on the same train of thought. "What about an old case you've closed? Did any of the perps threaten you? Have a spouse or sibling swear retribution?"

Shane added his two cents. "Do you have any open cases where the victim or a family member has threatened you if we don't get answers soon enough for them?"

Brian Stockman pulled his notepad out to jot down some information. "It would be easy enough to check who's out of prison now. Or who's still in—and could be getting help from the outside. I'll have Chelsea do some research."

Didn't that scenario sound familiar?

"I've already asked Chelsea to go through Noah Boggs's phone call and visitor log in South Carolina," Gray said.

"Allie's ex?"

Gray nodded. Brian made a note. "Good. We'll

extend that search to people you've helped put away here in Missouri."

Mac stood. Everyone else in the room closed ranks around him, sensing they were about to be given a mission to complete. "Priority one. Gray, I want you to scan through your cases and see if any suspects pop up. We still have other cases on the agenda but use anyone on your team who's available to help."

"And I want to run tests on that blood from the parking garage last night," Gray said. "The blood drops on that florist's card tested as human. I'm still stymied where our perp is getting that much blood to work with. The donors have to be identifiable. Either from a blood bank, a hospital or another crime."

"I can read your files," Jackson offered, "to free you up for the lab time."

"If we get a call to a crime scene, I'll pick up the slack with Lexi and Zoe," Shane added, "so you can stay on-site."

Mac ran the administrative end of the forensic department now, but he still knew how to work a crime scene. "Put my name on the call list, too, Brian, if their team needs the help. In the meantime, I'll look through the open cases, see if anyone looks particularly displeased with Malone."

Gray had lost his two best buddies to that RPG in the desert. He'd been sent home to heal and discharged from the Marines. With the military career he'd planned for his life no longer an option, he'd reinvented and reeducated himself as a criminalist. Although he understood about training himself to do a job, he'd missed the brotherhood, the certainty that whatever he had to do, he wouldn't be doing it alone. For the first time, he truly realized that he was still part of a team. The men around this table, and the women he worked with, too, were the people he wanted by his side in this fight. They might not wear combat gear and carry assault rifles. They weren't fighting a war against terrorism or helping political allies survive civil unrest. They were fighting a war on the home front. This team would help him uncover the truth. They would stop whoever was messing with Allie and bring the perp to justice.

They had his back on this mission to find the answers he needed.

They had Allie's, too.

GRAY SWORE AS he read the results of the printout. He should be happy that he'd finally found a match to the blood sample from the parking garage. But identifying the donor left him with more questions than answers. "Shaquina Carlyle? Who is that?"

Jackson pulled the laptop he was using closer and typed in a search, waiting far more patiently than Gray could for any results to show up. His eyes met Gray's above the equipment on the stainless-steel lab table separating them. "Missing person case."

Gray walked around the table to read the details over Jackson's shoulder. "Twenty-two-year-old female. Left work from a convenience store one night and never made it home."

"No viable leads. Looks like she got moved to Cold Case." Jackson rolled his stool to the side when Gray leaned forward to type in his own search parameters. "What are you thinking?" he asked in his deep, grumbly voice.

Gray adjusted himself back over his crutches, subconsciously remembering Allie's advice to use his core and balance over his legs. "I was going over the list of missing blood that Chelsea compiled for me."

"You said the only significant volume was from that hospital where the refrigeration unit went out and they had to dispose of the tainted blood supply. This missing person report was filed long before that incident." His arched brow asked Gray to explain what he was thinking.

Gray thought back to the basics of his scientific training. "None of the blood I've tested would be viable for a transfusion. The red blood cells lose their ability to produce oxygen after six weeks. But adding a disodium calcium complex and freezing it could make the supply last a lot longer, giving our perp time to accumulate it."

"Did you detect the preservation chemicals in your tests?"

Gray nodded. "Where else could our perp get his

hands on that much blood in the first place? There had to be a gallon or more used at Allie's place. That's almost as much as in one human body."

Jackson's brain went to the same dark place where Gray's had gone. "Serial killer." The big man sorted through the stack of closed case folders he'd been reading and pulled one out. He laid it open over the keyboard. "Like Jamie Kleinschmidt."

Gray nodded. "He drained the blood from his victims' bodies and stored it in his basement. There was a freezer full of the stuff in baby food jars from multiple victims. Took me weeks to get through it all. I could conclusively match the three victims he was convicted of killing. The other samples were too degraded, or I couldn't match them to any donor. The samples that weren't destroyed are still in our evidence storage facility. Chelsea confirmed that those are all accounted for."

"You think he had another stash somewhere?"

"Him or someone like him. Though, I haven't seen any indication that there's another bloodletter in KC."

"Kleinschmidt's dead."

No need to point out the obvious. "There goes my suspect list."

"Friends? Family? Fanatic?"

Retribution was a definite possibility. Kleinschmidt had been a disturbed young man who'd claimed his murders were a cleansing ritual—that he only killed sinners and whores. Gray's cool, thorough, scientific testimony on the witness stand had negated the emotional fears and sensationalism of the deaths inside the courtroom. But other zealots outside the courtroom had claimed he was a man with a divine purpose who was purging the ills of society. Of course, there had been just as many opponents arguing the victimization of women. In the end, Kleinschmidt, not interested in being a symbol for any cause and unable to stand the pressures of prison life where he was serving three life terms, had hanged himself in his prison cell. "I don't remember him having family there in the courtroom. Without any healthy support system, it's no wonder he was so unstable. And if there is a copycat, he's not killing the women—at least, we haven't had any dead bodies that show that kind of controlled exsanguination. Kleinschmidt used the funeral home where he worked to drain his victims. Started off by using legitimate corpses being embalmed or cremated by the mortuary. Until that wasn't enough, and he started hunting for new victims in no-man's-land."

Jackson frowned. "Most funeral homes upgraded their security after Kleinschmidt's trial."

"I haven't seen any reports of break-ins at funeral homes, either." Gray turned his focus back to the laptop as the information he sought scrolled on to the screen. "No reported bloodletting deaths in the KC area or outstate Missouri." He studied the grim facts, hoping they would reveal a lead he could follow. Just like with his military training—when the enemy blocked one route of attack, the team sought out another option. "Maybe instead of looking where blood is missing, we look at where that much blood can be stored."

"I'm on it." Jackson scooted back in front of his laptop while Gray picked up Jamie Kleinschmidt's file and carried it across the room to his desk where he woke his own laptop.

"Kleinschmidt always claimed there was more to his stash than what we found in his basement. That's how his lawyer got the death penalty off the table—there was always the hope that his client would reveal the identity and location of more of his victims." Gray skipped the KCPD databases and logged in to the county clerk's public access site to type in Kleinschmidt's last address. "So where has that blood been all this time? Did someone find it? Did someone keep it for him and is using it now?" The image of an empty, overgrown lot filled the screen. "The house where Kleinschmidt lived and kept his trophies has been demolished. Lot's for sale."

Jackson grunted. Yeah, it probably was hard to resell a house where a serial murderer had lived and kept his trophies.

"I don't see any other properties owned by Kleinschmidt." He'd have to call the Realtor selling the lot to see who the owner was. Maybe that person had run across a more secret stash of the killer's souvenirs. "We're certain he worked alone, right?"

"Your testimony, not mine," Jackson reminded him as he jotted down some possibilities from his research. "Wholesale storage caves along the river. Refrigerators at closed restaurants. An old butcher shop."

Gray nodded at the list where a perp could store a large quantity of blood that wasn't on any medical registry. "We could check utilities and see if any of those businesses are still generating electric bills." Gray typed in one more search. "I wonder if there was any vandalism of Kleinschmidt's house after he was arrested, and we cleared the evidence. If one of his fanatics who thought he was doing good work discovered something we missed, he could be using that blood to target me by terrorizing Allie." Yet another dead end. "No break-ins. No more jars of blood unearthed when the construction crew razed the house."

Scrubbing his hand over his cheeks and jaw, Gray leaned back in his chair. "Kleinschmidt's blood is a dead end for now." He stretched his arms out, easing the tension in his shoulders. "How long have we been at this?"

Jackson grunted at the joke as Gray eyed the clock. It was after five. Time to wrap things up and get over to the clinic to pick up Allie. She'd be pleased that he'd worn his legs all day, but he was feeling the strain. He felt the beginnings of a smile relax the corners of his mouth. Maybe since he'd been a good boy and had listened to her advice, she would massage his back tonight. He'd be happy to return the favor. Or maybe he could convince her to rub the therapeutic lotion into his thighs again tonight.

Allie hadn't freaked out when she'd seen the scarred skin last night after he'd changed into a pair of shorts for sleeping. In fact, she'd been the one to ask permission if she could touch him. No one but medical professionals and his own hands had touched his legs since the last operation. Certainly not Brittany. And no other woman except the nurses when he was in the hospital. Allie's hands had been gentle, yet strong, easing the discomfort of ravaged skin and overtaxed muscles without hurting him.

His eyes drifted shut and he imagined her hands massaging other places. There was nothing broken or missing in his body's reaction to her touch. Nerve endings sparked to life just thinking about it. A hunger pooled in his belly. His fingers danced with the desire to bury themselves in her long, silky hair. His manhood twitched with the need to bury himself inside her. He'd be awkward as an untried teenager making love to Allie. And he had a feeling being with her would be just as memorable as that first time he'd made love. No, it would be even better, because it would be Allie's soft blue-gray eyes he'd be looking into. It would be her sweet, strong body clinging to his. He knew without a doubt that his Navy lieutenant would make him feel like a whole, desirable man, even as he did his damnedest to please her in whatever way he could.

Gray heard Jackson clearing his throat and he realized he'd taken a mental vacation for a few minutes. Jackson's gaze shifted to the cell phone sitting on the desk beside Gray's laptop, and he realized he'd been pinged with a text.

Gray eagerly picked up his phone and unlocked it. It was probably Allie joking about losing track of the time, begging him to rescue her from a recalcitrant patient, or even making simple small talk about what they'd have for dinner.

He frowned when he saw the number.

Not Allie. Something worse.

He was already dialing when he read Ben Hunter's message.

Call me.

The moment Ben picked up, Gray spoke. "Is Allie okay?"

"She's not hurt."

The unspoken message was that something else was terribly wrong. Gray should feel relieved that she was in one piece, but his racing pulse was pounding with alarm. He grabbed his crutches and pushed to his feet. "Another threat?"

"You need to get here. It's not good."

Anchoring the phone between his ear and shoulder, Gray hooked his crutches on to each forearm. "I need details, Sergeant."

Gray was aware of Jackson closing his laptop and rising like a leviathan from his side of the table.

The Army sergeant who'd claimed he could do reconnaissance and watch over Allie at the clinic gave a concise, if worrisome, report. "She's locked the door to the staff locker room and won't come out. She won't talk to me. To anyone. I didn't think I should break down the door."

"I'm on my way."

Hiding was the last thing Gray expected his Allie to do. She was the one who armed herself with pepper spray and guarded his six when he checked out the break-in at her apartment. She was the one who ignored her fears and answered every question the police put to her. She was the one who pushed when he wanted to retreat, who shut down lecherous coworkers with a sharp word, and who faced off against a superior officer in a court of law to make sure the truth was heard. Allie Tate might need to hold his hand or walk by his side or share his kiss to bolster her courage, but she didn't lock herself in a room and shut herself away from the problem at hand. What could have happened?

Gray wished he could snap his fingers and be there for her instantly. He'd have to settle for putting the portable siren on top of his van and racing to the clinic as fast as traffic would allow. Ben was right. This wasn't good. "If the situation changes and you hear any signs of distress, break down the door."

"Understood."

Apparently, the one-handed Army sergeant wasn't into goodbyes and Gray didn't need one.

Jackson asked, "Need help?"

Gray strode to the door as quickly as his legs and crutches allowed. Style wasn't a consideration. "Text Allie. Text her until she answers. I can't walk and text at the same time. Tell her I'm coming. I'll drive."

Jackson took the phone and fell into step beside him. "I'll notify the team where we're headed."

Despite rush hour traffic, Gray made the drive to the PT clinic in ten minutes. He didn't care that he'd lurched to a stop with the front right wheel up on the curb. He didn't care that a small crowd was gathering in the lobby. He didn't care that the only response Jackson had gotten was an OK acknowledging the texts.

What he cared about was that Allie was in trouble. But was she too independent, or too terrified, to reach out to him for help?

With Jackson following behind him, Gray spotted Ben Hunter through the front door and hurried to meet him. "Report."

Ben fell into step with him. "No change. She cussed at me the last time I asked if she was all right. Something about it being safer for everyone and to go away."

"You're certain she wasn't hurt?"

"She wasn't the last time I saw her. She seemed happy. Joked a little about me being hairier than her regular shadow. She said she was done for the day, grabbing her stuff and heading out front to wait for you." Ben pushed open the lobby door into the clinic room. "Next thing I knew, she was bolting the door."

When they entered the clinic's treatment area, Doug Friesen stepped away from the hallway wall to greet them. He thumbed over his shoulder to the closed door of the staff's changing room. "She's gone all diva on us. Won't talk to anyone. Some of us would like to get in there and get our stuff so we can go home. If she makes me late for my date..."

With a lightning-swift move his combat training sergeant would have admired, Gray thrust his forearm across Friesen's clavicle and shoved him back up against the wall. "Did you say or do anything to her?"

"Lighten up, Loverboy." Friesen tugged at the arm braced across his chest. But with the full weight of Gray's body leaning into him, the other man couldn't escape. As usual, he let his big, annoying mouth do the talking. "You know, she's been nothing but trouble since she started working here."

"She's trouble because she hasn't fallen for your cheap lines and unwanted touches?"

"Like her last boyfriend? I heard she caused a stink there, too, after he dumped her. Got him into serious trouble."

"He tried to kill her." Gray enunciated the fact right in Friesen's face.

He felt a restraining hand fold over his shoulder and heard Jackson's voice in his ear. "Priorities."

Right. Friesen and his sneering misinformation didn't matter. Getting to Allie did.

Gray held both hands up as he released Friesen and backed away. The other man adjusted his wrinkled polo shirt and slid out of Gray's way. "I see you brought your whole posse with you. If it was just you and me, Malone, this conversation would have a different ending."

Ignoring the taunt, Gray followed the direction of Ben's hook, pointing to the closed door. "In there."

Gray nodded his thanks. The surly veteran had done exactly as he'd asked of him. "Sergeant, secure this back area. No one else comes in until I say so. Jackson, have my kit ready." He looked beyond his friend's shoulder and eyed the crowd of staff and patients who had shifted into the end of the hallway. He spotted the worried frown on Maeve Phillips's face. "Ma'am, if there's anything you can do to divert attention away from whatever's happening with Allie, I'd appreciate it."

The curly-haired brunette nodded. "Of course, I'll get the rest of the staff to help me." She nudged the coworker still brooding beside her. "Move, Doug. You may be off the clock, but you still work here."

"Man, she's rubbing off on you, too. Not a compliment." When Ben and Jackson added their considerable glares to back up Maeve, Friesen snorted his protest before fixing a smile on his face and turning to a group of patients. "Come on, folks."

Maeve glanced back to meet Gray's gaze. "Tell her I'm worried about her. We'll take care of things out here."

He gave the young woman a curt nod, then turned his full attention on the locked door. He knocked. "Allie? It's Gray. I need you to let me in." When there wasn't any answer, he knocked again, a little more forcefully. "Lieutenant. I don't want you to be alone."

He couldn't detect any movement until he heard Allie's voice from the other side of the door. "Just you?"

Thank God she was responding to him. "Just me."

The lock turned and the door opened just wide enough for him to step in. He took a couple of steps past her as she relocked the door behind him. When he turned to face her, she walked into his chest. She cinched her arms around his waist and rested her forehead against the juncture of his neck and shoulder. She breathed in deeply, once, twice. Her chest expanded with a third deep breath, and she seemed to relax a bit as he closed his arms around her and dipped his nose to her hair to nuzzle her temple. She didn't seem to mind that his crutches were dangling against her backside. She simply aligned her body to his as if he was some kind of healing therapy she needed to concentrate on for a few minutes.

Still with no clue as to what had happened, Gray swept his gaze around the room. Typical locker room. Walls lined with lockers. Benches in front of the lockers. Two bathroom doors. A rolling basket filled with used towels. Her cheek felt chilled against him, but he couldn't detect her shivering. She wasn't crying. He hadn't spotted any blood on her clothes or marks on her face or hands. The only thing that looked out of place was the gray-and-red hoodie he'd loaned her lying in a heap on the floor in front of an open locker.

It was his nature to process the details around him, but he needed context for any of this to make sense. When he felt her posture shift slightly, some of her strength returning, he spoke. "Allie?"

"I know. Talk to you. I didn't want anyone in here in case you wanted to process it. And..." Her breath gusted with a weary sigh. "I'm just peopled out."

He hoped he'd picked up on the important information here. "Process what?"

He felt a quick kiss to the angle of his jaw before she stepped back and pointed to the open locker. "In there."

"Yours?" he asked.

She snorted a laugh that held no humor. "Who else?"

Gray automatically pulled his sterile gloves from the pocket of his jeans and moved around the bench to inspect the open locker more closely. *Please don't let there be more blood.* The woman had already been surrounded by far too much of it. He made a visual sweep of the standard metal locker. No graffiti. No obvious signs of tampering with the lock. Her skinny purse with the long strap hung from a hook. He saw the sweatpants, T-shirt and running shoes sticking out of a tote bag that sat on the bottom shelf. From this angle, he could see a blank white envelope on the floor beneath his jacket.

She moved in behind him, keeping the width of the bench between them. "On the top shelf. I haven't been in there since changing this morning. It wasn't there then."

Glad he had his legs on so he could easily see the top shelf, Gray noted that there were only two items—a pack of gum and a key. Shiny and new and recently made, he had a sick feeling he recognized that key. He needed to remain calm. She needed him to be a criminalist. "What am I looking at?"

"A key to my apartment. Possibly the one 'Payback' used to get inside. Who knows how many copies he made?" She hugged her arms around her waist. "I checked. The original is still on my keychain."

One small key. Clearly a taunt. Gray reached back

to cup the side of Allie's face and neck. It felt wrong to have his sterile glove separating her soft skin from his touch, but she didn't seem to mind. "You're not going back to your apartment. You're staying with me. You don't even have to look inside your place until Aiden or Officer Cutler and I clear it for ourselves." With her understanding nod, he turned back and closed the locker door most of the way. "The perp could have slipped the envelope through the grates at the top of your locker. He wouldn't have to know the combination or force it open." He was working, thinking like a criminalist. It was the best way to help her right now. He glanced up to the corners of the room. "There are security cameras in the main room to monitor the patients' well-being. Are they back here, too?"

"No. Whoever stuck that in my locker wasn't caught on tape."

"That means a staff member put it there." Although his thoughts immediately went to Doug Friesen, who seemed like he would enjoy upsetting Allie, Gray was too well trained to rule out any possibility. "An outsider could have asked someone on staff to do them the favor of delivering it. Gave them some story about how you lost or forgot your key. The patient himself could sneak back here if the room was unlocked. Anyone who could get past the lobby could…" But when he saw how hard she was hugging herself and could clearly see her shivering as she stared into the locker, Gray got into her space. He rubbed some warmth into her upper arms, and ducked his head to look her in the eye. "Babe, you need to talk to me right now."

Her gaze didn't shy away from his. "Maybe this *is* about you. About *us*. I'm sorry I ever got you into this mess."

"I'm not." He would never regret meeting this woman, becoming friends, falling in love with her. He couldn't say what the future between them looked like, couldn't guarantee they had one, but he would never regret loving Allie. She'd reminded him he was a man. She'd taught him he had value beyond being a forensic chemist or a survivor. She challenged him to become whatever she needed him to be. He searched the locker again. "The key was in the envelope?"

"Read the note."

"The note?"

"I dropped it so I wouldn't contaminate any evidence you might find on it. And…" Whatever she'd seen had shut her down. "I just needed to get away from it."

"I'll find it." He found the folded note card behind the tote bag in the bottom of her locker where it had fallen. Irregular red dots decorated the outside. Recognizing blood spatter, Grayson cursed. Allie had taken a direct hit to any sense of security she had left. He read the blood-spotted note.

Noah sends his regards. He's not happy that you've gotten involved with another man. He wants me to send him a sample of YOUR blood when I'm finished with you. Give my regards to your boyfriend. He'll suffer as much as you when you're gone.

Payback will be complete.

Chapter Eleven

"You're sure you want to do this?" Allie asked, her gaze darting from Grayson's friend Aiden Murphy to Aiden's K-9 partner, Blue.

"Blue and I work out every day," Aiden assured her, tucking his KCPD T-shirt into his running pants and double-checking the small gun secured in a holster around his ankle. "Sometimes, it's agility work or patrol training, followed by play—and sometimes, it's a good old-fashioned run. As long as he's busy and gets his Kong to play with or a tummy rub at the end, he's a happy camper."

Happy indeed. The Belgian Malinois watched his partner's every move, possibly waiting for the signal to go, while his tail thumped with rapid excitement against Gray's front door. "I've been doing this for years," Allie felt compelled to point out. "Ran cross-country in high school and college. I take things at a pretty fast pace."

"We can keep up." It wasn't that she doubted the

blue-eyed officer's fitness, or that of the muscular K-9 who was wagging his whole butt now.

But she couldn't help but remember how Bubba Summerfield had intruded on her run yesterday morning. She didn't do this for chitchat or introspection. She ran to get away from the mind games that were closing in all around her and suffocating her with fear. She hated being afraid. She wanted to clear her head enough so that she could seize the anger she felt inside her, as well. She'd been targeted once before because she was a strong woman who wouldn't back down from the wrong man. Now her world was spiraling out of control again—and she'd made Gray a target, too. The note in her locker yesterday had indicated that making Gray suffer was part of this creep's plan, as well.

She was getting too used to having a man she relied on to be there for her, too used to sharing meals and daily conversations, too used to sleeping on Gray's couch with his strong arms curled around her. If anything happened to him because of her, she'd never forgive herself.

Aiden stooped down to tighten the knot on his shoe and fended off Blue's eager tongue. He pushed the dog away and stood, apparently ready to go. "Besides, I don't think Malone is going to let you out of his sight unless Blue and me are with you."

"Malone doesn't want her to go at all." A third voice joined the conversation. It was early enough in the morning that Gray hadn't put on his prosthetic legs yet. He rolled his chair over to the entryway and reached for her hand and squeezed, silently telling her that despite his protective instincts, he understood that she needed to do this. Running was her therapy, the way she cleared her mind and got her heart pumping hard enough to reset her strength against the malaise her stalker created in her. It was probably killing him that he couldn't do this run with her. "I owe ya one, Murph."

"No, you don't." Aiden shrugged off the offer. "It's what friends do. You guys are the team Lexi always wanted to work with at the lab. She trusts you and values your respect in return. She feels safe to go to work again, with you and Dobbs and Chels and Shane, Buck and Rufus and Mac there to back her up. I don't take that lightly."

Gray nodded. "I don't take you having Allie's back this morning lightly, either. This is important to her."

When she felt his gaze drift up to her, Allie leaned down and kissed him. "We'll be back within the hour."

He caught her ponytail in his hand and let it sift through his fingers. "I'll have breakfast ready and drive you to the clinic when you're done."

Grayson Malone showed more understanding than she'd ever expected from a man. More caring than she probably deserved, because there'd been nothing but trouble in her life since they'd grown closer to each other. "Thank you." Those piercing green eyes caressed her very soul as she pulled away, keeping them connected in a way that filled every lonely spot inside her. "Gray, I..."

The words *I love you* danced on her tongue. She felt them in her heart. But with everything that had happened over the past few days, she couldn't quite wrap her brain around the idea Grayson Malone was the man she'd been hoping to find. How much of what she was feeling was gratitude or a craving for the emotional security he provided? He might be what she needed, but was she what *he* needed? Had circumstances forced them together and elicited feelings that had blossomed in the heat of the moment? Could the love she felt be real?

"I'll see you soon," she said instead, offering him a genuine smile.

He nodded and held the door as Aiden opened it and Blue tugged him down the hallway. "Keep her safe, Murph," Gray called after his friend.

"Will do."

Gray caught her hand one more time before she exited after her running partners. "Keys? Pepper spray? Phone?"

Allie giggled. "Yes, Dad."

But Gray didn't laugh. "Come back to me."

Allie nearly stumbled over her own feet at the stark request. She cupped the side of his jaw and leaned down to kiss the corner of his mouth. "Always."

Admitting out loud how much she wanted to be with Gray was probably more of a surprise to her than it was to him. But Allie didn't stop to evaluate what they'd inadvertently admitted to each other. She needed a little time to process the depth of what was happening between them. They'd both been hurt so badly in the past that she didn't want to make a mistake and hurt either Gray or herself.

Besides, this was her running time. Not time for thinking. Not time for feeling. Not time for stress. Time simply to be free.

She jogged down the hall to join Aiden and Blue on the elevator. When she turned to watch the door close, she saw Gray in his wheelchair in the middle of the hallway, watching until she disappeared from sight.

MORNING RUSH HOUR traffic was getting thicker and the air was getting smoggy as Allie jogged at a fast clip along the sidewalks around the Western Auto building and headed back up the hill toward Crown Center and the World War I Memorial. Even with a streetcar system and overhead walkways installed to reduce commuter traffic and encourage walkers, cyclists and public transportation, there were plenty of delivery vans and carpools and drivers funneling into downtown KC off the highways that the relaxed feeling of the first thirty minutes of her run was quickly dissipating.

She kept her eyes peeled for the stream of pedestrians filtering out of parking garages and bus stops and tramcars onto the sidewalk ahead of her. She tried to keep to the left side near the curb to allow the slower walkers plenty of space so that she didn't mow anyone down or announce herself to the people who veered in front of her. As long as she could see the people ahead of her and avoid getting caught at the line of traffic waiting to pull into their reserved parking garages for the day, she wouldn't have to make conversation with anyone. She could concentrate on the rhythm of her feet hitting the pavement, check her watch and pulse periodically, and monitor her breathing. She was on the homebound leg of her run, and she was right on track to make it back to the apartment building in the forty to forty-five minutes she'd promised Gray.

She was aware of Aiden and Blue jogging the same path about half a block behind her. True to his word, the K-9 cop and his Belgian Malinois had no trouble keeping the pace Allie had set. And he'd been fine with her concept for solitude on the condition that she stay in visual range and do exactly as he ordered if he spotted anyone or anything that looked like a threat. Since Noah and his copycat associate seemed to thrive more on sneaking around the fringes of her life without showing themselves, she doubted Aiden would spot the mystery man who'd been tormenting her. But she understood rules and security protocols. She wasn't putting herself out there as bait. If Aiden said duck or run faster, she'd do exactly that.

In the meantime, she was going to exhaust her body and recharge her brain and hurry home to Gray.

Even as the thought struck her that there were more vehicles and pedestrians than she would have expected to see downtown on a Saturday morning, she nearly plowed into a door opening beside the curb. "Sorry!" she shouted, darting around the obstacle. When it registered that the woman getting out had had green sparkly hair, she remembered that there was a convention in town up at Bartle Hall. Suddenly, she focused in on the pedestrians who had been a blur in her peripheral vision. Men and women, children and even pets were in costumes reflecting various movie franchises and what she suspected were anime characters from graphic novels or video games.

Of course, she'd picked the weekend for one of the biggest conventions in the Midwest to assert her independence. *Not smart, Lieutenant.* If she had thought about the convention, she could at least have picked a less public route through the city. She'd mistakenly thought she'd be safer with more people around her and fewer places for the stranger stalking her to hide. But apparently, until the convention opened for its morning sessions, the streets and sidewalks would be packed with people waiting to go inside Bartle Hall.

When Allie reached the next traffic light she stopped at the crosswalk and turned, hoping to catch a glimpse of Aiden and discuss a different, less populous path they could take back to her apartment building. Still jogging in place to keep her heart rate up, and thankful she was taller than a lot of the people surrounding her, she scanned a horde of placards and costumes being steadily fed by the patrons of the convention gathering at the same intersection.

It took her a few seconds to spot Aiden, who had stopped farther up the sidewalk to answer a question or give directions to a group of women dressed in sparkly fairy costumes. When she caught his eye, she waved and pointed across the street, hoping he'd get the message that she wanted to alter their course away from the crowd. She supposed she should shoot him a text to explain her concern and suggest an alternative. But when he gave her a thumbs-up, she pushed her phone back into the pocket of her sweats and changed course to cross the opposite direction.

Her timing sucked as the light chose that moment to change and the crowd that had gathered behind her surged forward. Allie uttered her fair share of *excuse me's* as she pushed her way to the side and found herself waiting at yet another traffic light.

As a woman, she tried to always be aware of her surroundings. Yes, she could defend herself if she had to. Chances were that she could outrun most people who tried to pursue her on foot. But that was when she was at 100 percent. As a woman being stalked, she didn't feel 100 percent. Her stalker's mind games were wearing her down in a way that being targeted by Noah hadn't. Maybe she wasn't fully recovered from surviving her ex, and she hadn't been ready to take on another subversive enemy so soon. Maybe knowing that "Payback" knew about Grayson, and had sent that convoluted message about making him suffer as well, had thrown her off her game. She was distracted. Missing the signs of danger and intrusion on her life. Second-guessing the observations and choices she did make.

Maybe that was why the black car that had pulled up to the stop light beside her didn't immediately register. And now that she was aware of how it had changed two lanes of traffic to claim a parking spot across the street shortly after she had signaled Aiden and changed directions, she questioned the vague memory that the car looked familiar. Was she just imprinting Bubba's description of a car that had been watching her and Gray on to the vehicle? She remembered the car that had nearly run them down in the parking garage across from the clinic had been black. But was every black car a threat?

She listened to her first instinct and studied the car while she waited. Black, four-door sedan. She couldn't see the license plate. She couldn't see a parking permit sticker on the windshield. But then, the absence of a sticker was hardly a help when it came to identifying a car, considering there were more cars without stickers in Kansas City than with. Its tinted windows meant she couldn't see the driver. Also no help. And no one was getting out of the car.

Her pulse rate slowed as she felt her body cooling down, and knew she needed to get moving soon, or she'd lose her momentum and have to build up speed and her breathing rate again. Did she go back to Aiden for help? Continue her run? Stand here in overthinking paranoia until the next troupe of conventioneers swarmed around her and carried her away in the flow of pedestrian traffic?

"It's just a black car," she whispered to herself. "You have Aiden and Blue with you. There are hundreds of witnesses around here if something does go wrong." When the crosswalk light hit zero and the light changed, Allie latched on to the confidence wavering inside her. With a quick wave to Aiden to make sure he saw where she was headed, she stepped into the street and jogged across, lengthening her stride into a run when her feet hit the opposite sidewalk.

Her nostrils flared as she took in a deep breath. Noah hadn't broken her. "Payback" wouldn't, either.

She was inhaling the fragrant aromas coming from the coffee shop on the corner when she heard a woman scream. Allie slowed her pace and glanced over her shoulder as tires squealed on pavement and horns honked. A dozen costumed people were yelling and pushing and pulling each other back from the crosswalk as the same black car careened around the corner. With the grid of one-way streets in downtown KC, the car pulled into the left lane right next to the sidewalk where she was running. The driver stomped on his brakes as he neared her. There was nothing between her and the driver behind the tinted windows besides the row of parked cars at the curb as he slowed to keep pace with her.

This time, Allie didn't ignore the alarm bells clanging inside her head. She pulled her cell phone from her pocket and punched in Aiden's number. When she increased her speed, the car kept pace with her. When she passed the void of an alley, the black car swerved slightly into the empty space, and she jumped back against the gray brick of the building behind her.

The car was going much too fast to make the turn and swerved back out, scraping the bumper of the car in front of it. As the vehicle raced on down the street, Allie shifted direction and sprinted back toward the convention center.

Aiden picked up. "What's up?"

"I'm being followed."

Her friendly fellow runner was all cop now. "Where are you? There are too many people. I've lost sight of you."

"I'm doubling back toward Wyandotte."

"You need to get out of sight."

"He's in a car heading the opposite direction now. He has to stay in the street, right? I'm hugging the buildings so he can't get to me."

Another chorus of horns blared behind her, and she turned to see the black car screeching around in a U-turn and weaving back up the street against oncoming traffic.

Not her imagination.

Allie swore like a sailor. "He turned around. He's going the wrong way."

She ran through a crowd of people and heard their comments.

"That guy's going to cause an accident."

"Is he drunk?"

"He's crazy."

Aiden was slightly breathless as he ran, or maybe that was the sound of Blue panting beside him. "Describe the car. License?"

"If there's a plate, I can't see it. It's black. Tinted windows."

"Like the one in the parking garage?"

"Possibly."

"KCPD! Police officer! Get out of my way!" She imagined he was shouting a warning to the people or drivers who were in his way. Then he was talking to her again. "We're coming to you. Get to the coffee shop on the corner. Go inside."

Wait. A crowd of people? Allie's pace stuttered. "But all these people—"

"Negative. Backup is on the way. Get to safety."

Metal crunched against metal behind her. The warning complaints of all the horns was nearly deafening. Rubber screeched against pavement. There were police sirens filling the air now. He just kept coming.

After her. He kept coming after her.

And she was in the middle of all these innocent people.

Allie waved her arms in the air. "Everybody needs to get away from the street!" She grabbed a woman's arm and pulled her away from the curb. "Get inside! Get out of his way!"

"Allie!"

The woman and her friends screamed and cursed, but they were moving.

"Stop!" she shouted, warning the group entering the crosswalk to retreat. "Get off the street!"

Then someone shouted, "Look out!"

Allie caught a glimpse of Aiden at the top of the street before she spun around and saw the black car jump the curb and barrel into the alley where she'd stopped. She swore she felt the heat of a dragon's breath singeing her back as she ran as fast as her long legs could go. She wove back and forth, trying to stay ahead of it. The black car exploded through a pile of trash bags and scraped the side of a loading dock before Allie figured out her escape.

Her heart pounding against her ribs and her lungs gasping for air, she ran up the steps of the next loading dock and threw herself against the metal door there. It didn't budge. "Damn it!" Of course, it was locked. With all these extra people in the neighborhood, the business couldn't risk an intruder sneaking in the back.

Before she could come up with a plan B, the black car swerved past the loading dock toward the far end of the alley. But the driver overcorrected the turn and bounced off the wall of the other building. The car scraped along the bricks, shooting up sparks until it plowed into the next concrete loading dock. The front end crumpled, and the air bags inflated as steam instantly clouded up from under the hood.

Although she could barely hear herself think over the pulse hammering in her ears and the continuous blare of the car's horn, her training as a medical professional kicked in and she climbed back down to the pavement. The combination of off-the-charts adrenaline crashing through her body and her heavy breathing after that life-saving sprint made her a little light-headed. She swayed for a moment and had to lean against the stair railing for a few seconds to regain her equilibrium before she could check on the driver.

She heard someone shouting her name through her muffled hearing as she pushed away from the railing. Then the car door opened and a man fell out onto his hands and knees.

"Are you all right?" she called to him. "Who are you? Why are you doing this?"

Instead of answering, the man pulled the ball cap he wore low over his dark hair. He lurched to his feet and pulled the collar of his jacket up to his chin without ever looking back.

When she realized he was leaving the crash, Allie tried to run. "Stop! Why are you doing this to me?"

There were other voices behind her, shouting for

the man to stop. He staggered a few steps, then found his bearings and sped into a jog, disappearing around the corner onto the street before she reached the car.

Realizing what she thought was steam was actually smoke and that the car was now a fire hazard, Allie leaned inside the open car door to turn off the ignition. As soon as she pulled her hand away from the tarnished silver key ring, she froze. Memories buffeted her like a punch to the gut and she instinctively retreated.

Into the hands of Aiden Murphy. "Don't touch anything!"

With a startled yelp, she spun around.

"You okay?" he asked, dipping his head to assess her eyes.

Allie put up her hands, telling him she knew who he was and she was fine. "He didn't hit me. I climbed up on one of the loading docks…" Why hadn't he run her down? Was she really that fast a runner? Had something changed his mind at the last second?

"Smart thinking." Aiden squeezed her shoulder. He could barely contain Blue, who was straining against his leash. "Where's the driver?"

"He took off on foot. That way."

With a curt nod, Aiden pulled away. "All right. Blue can track him. Backup is on the way. You call Gray." When she didn't immediately respond, he squeezed her shoulder again. "You okay if I leave you?"

Get your head in the game, Lieutenant! Understanding speed was of the essence if Aiden had any chance of catching the driver, Allie nodded and pulled out her phone. "Calling Gray."

"Blue. *Such!*" Aiden gave the dog a sharp order in German, and then he and Blue jogged down the alley and turned right onto the sidewalk.

Still wondering how the impossible could be true, Allie ignored the concerned citizens and curiosity seekers making their way down the alley and coming out of shop doors and leaned back inside the car. She realized now there was blood on the steering wheel. The windshield was a spider web of cracks and there was an indistinct, bloody handprint on the dashboard.

But her gaze was focused on the keys again. Only two keys—the one in the ignition with a few drops of blood on it and another hanging from the metal ring. But it was the key ring itself that was speaking to her, haunting her. A round bangle of silver with the letter B carved into its matte finish.

B.

Boggs.

She snapped a picture of it with her phone and retreated to the far side of the alley to pull up Gray's number.

Noah had a keychain like that. She'd bought one exactly like it for a birthday present for him on their fifth and last date. A trinket from a souvenir stand at an amusement park. She thought it was fun. He thought it was cheap, said he'd spent a hell of a lot more on her just to get them into the park.

She squeezed her eyes shut and shook her head before opening them again. Maybe she was dreaming. Maybe something in her had finally snapped and she really was losing her mind. She was surrounded by a crowd of aliens and time lords and cartoon characters. She was looking at more blood.

And Noah Boggs's keychain.

THE DRIVER PULLED away from the curb into traffic almost before the passenger closed the door behind him. The passenger was breathing heavily and stinking up the car with his fetid breath.

"I'm bleeding." He pulled a tissue from his pocket, held it up to his nose and tipped his head back. "I didn't think it was going to hurt that much."

"Did you leave the souvenir as I instructed?"

"You know I did. I've done everything you told me to. I even told the lies you wanted me to almost word for word." He moaned like a toddler with a stubbed toe. Children in distress had always been something to be avoided. The sound was even more annoying in an adult. "Didn't you hear what I said? I controlled the crash, but I still got hurt. And man, that was a sweet car. I wouldn't mind driving one like that for real. It was a shame to bust it up like that."

And now the complaints started.

"You said you wanted to be more than my eyes on the woman when I hired you. I'll let you have your time with her. But only on my terms. And that doesn't include giving you a new car." The passenger's help was vital to completing this plan, and he'd been a willing, even eager, participant thus far. But one could wish for someone who didn't question or complain about every little thing. The driver reached into a bag and handed a towel to the man across the seat. "Use this for that nosebleed." After being so careful with transporting the blood from the refrigerator to each of Allie Tate's gifts, it wouldn't do to have this man's blood leaving trace in the car. "I'll get you fixed up. Is it just your nose, or have you cut something?"

The passenger sounded like he had a head cold as he spoke through the muffling of the towel. "You don't understand. My blood is now at that crash site. They can trace it back to me. That's what Malone does at the crime lab."

The driver curbed impatience as they slowed with the rest of the traffic crawling through downtown. Two police officers on bicycles wove through the stalled traffic while a black-and-white unit wailed its siren as it passed by. "Is your DNA in the system?"

The passenger turned his head to the side and adjusted his ball cap to hide more of his face. Not that it was necessary with the car's tinted windows. Besides, it was highly doubtful the police would give either of them a second look when they were focused on responding to the scene of the crash and crowd control. "Yeah, it is. I was in the military. They take samples from everyone in case they have to identify our remains."

The crime lab might have to put that particular piece of information to use when all this was said and done. But the driver told the passenger what he wanted to hear.

"Then we'll have to finish this before the boyfriend can trace that blood back to you." Moving up the timetable wasn't an issue. Allie Tate was primed for the final act. Then, retribution would be complete. "You'll be in the Cayman Islands or wherever you want to take your money before that happens."

"When do I get to hurt her?"

The driver laughed. "When I say so. And not a moment before. I need the stage set for everything to play out just as I planned. I won't be satisfied until then."

Chapter Twelve

Gray pulled his van into the alley and parked behind the CSIU van where Jackson and Shane were taping off the area around the wrecked car. Lexi was in a conversation with the driver of the tow truck parked at the opposite end of the alley, while Aiden was nearby, playing that silly reward game with the hard plastic toy his dog loved so much.

Although his training told him to head straight to the black car to start collecting the blood Lexi reported finding inside, Gray spotted Allie sitting on the steps of a concrete loading dock. Her long ponytail fell over her shoulder as she concentrated on whatever she was reading on her phone. After acknowledging Shane's and Jackson's greetings, Gray headed straight for the bowed head of honey-gold hair.

She heard his awkward steps crunching over the gravel and looked up. The moment their eyes met, she launched herself off the steps. Gray stopped, bracing himself. But Allie made it easy to keep his balance by slowing the last couple of strides, sliding her arms around his waist and snuggling against his neck. He released his grip on his crutches and held on to her, instead, dipping his nose to the crown of her hair and pressing his lips against her forehead. She felt good plastered against him, holding on as if his arrival was exactly what she needed. "Easy. You okay?"

He hadn't seen any blood on her. She wasn't limping or holding anything as if she was in pain, but he needed to know she wasn't hurt.

She nodded, clutching him tightly. "Better now. He was definitely following me. He did a U-ey and drove the wrong way up a one-way street when I changed directions. It could be the same car from the parking garage, but I'm not sure. You don't have to be mad or feel guilty about me running this morning. Aiden was right with me. No one got hurt." She glanced back toward the black car. "Well, except for the driver. There's blood inside the car, and Lexi says the trail of blood drops goes all the way out to the sidewalk."

"I'm not mad at you." He feathered his fingers into her hair and stroked it down against her back. "And I'm doing my damnedest not to feel guilty because I know there's no way I could have stopped you. You tend to have a stubborn streak."

Her giggle vibrated against the skin above the collar of his T-shirt. "And I really was feeling better until

I realized I—and all the innocent bystanders he could have hit—were in danger." She wasn't smiling when she unwound herself from his body and pulled up a picture on her cell phone. "Look at this. I wonder if he crashed the car on purpose. Just so I could find it."

Gray dropped his gaze to the image from the interior of the car. The pattern of blood droplets on the steering wheel and column indicated a pooling injury with drips of blood, not the spray of an impact injury. Chances were the driver had broken his nose or split open his forehead. The pressure of his hand, or even his face against the steering wheel, had stanched the blood flow until he released the pressure. But Gray doubted that was what she wanted to show him. "What am I looking at?"

"The keys. B. Noah Boggs." She was adamant as she tapped her phone to enlarge the image carved into the silvery disk. "I know this is his key ring because I gave it to him."

Gray frowned because she'd been traumatized enough to believe the impossible. He was a scientist. He needed evidence to believe what she was telling him. "Boggs is in prison, Allie. Chelsea and the NAVCONBRIG CHASN commandant confirmed it."

"Who else do I know whose name starts with B? Ben Hunter? Bubba Summerfield?" Did she really think this was the clue that would break the case wide open? That her stalker must be someone with B in their name because of the key ring?

"Brittany Carter."

Her eyes widened like saucers, then narrowed with a frown. "Your ex? I've never met her. Why would she want to hurt me?"

"If you're grasping at straws, then so am I." Gray snapped his fingers, pointing out how unfounded her suspicions were in an effort to help her think clearly again. "Mrs. Burroughs at the clinic."

"A self-important old woman with a limp is not lurking in the shadows terrorizing me." Allie swiped the image off her phone before tucking her cell into the pocket of her hoodie. "Maybe Noah sent the key ring to someone, and the driver left it behind with the intention that I'd see it."

"Maybe Doug Friesen changed his name."

"Did he?"

"I have no idea. And neither do you. Take a breath, Allie." She paused for a moment before doing just that. "And another." He saw that the moment the irrational panic left her eyes they softened to their beautiful color. "Stay in the here and now with me." His crutches dangled from the crook of his elbows as he gently framed her face between his hands. "This guy is not making you crazy. He's making you mad. Understand? He's not scaring you. He's forcing you to be smarter and stronger than he could ever hope to be."

Allie nodded, getting the point of his pep talk. She latched on to his wrists and held his gaze. "He's not isolating me. He's driving me closer to a man I care a great deal about, a man who I believe will fight by my side any day of the week."

"He will," Gray promised before leaning in and pressing a brief kiss to her lips. She kept hold of his hand when he stepped back and glanced at his friends from the crime lab and KCPD who had gathered around them. "You've got more allies and friends in your camp now than you ever had before. Plus, Maeve at work. Ben." Aiden released his dog and the Belgian Malinois ran between the two of them to nuzzle where their hands were joined. "Blue."

"I know you're not Mr. B." Allie scratched Blue around the ears and Gray patted his warm flanks. Content that he'd been suitably rewarded for his friendly overture, Blue trotted back to Aiden's side.

Aiden ordered his partner into a sit. "Blue tracked the driver's scent until it went cold. Not too far from the end of the alley. Witnesses say he got into another car. Passenger seat. They drove away."

"He has an accomplice?" Gray asked.

Aiden nodded. "That's probably how he's getting everything done without getting caught. One can drive while the other throws the blood out the window. Two people could get your apartment painted in a lot less time with less chance of being noticed."

"One could create a diversion while the other

sneaks into the locker room." Allie realized another probability. "There was no way for anyone to know I was running this morning." She looked up at Gray. "You and I didn't discuss it until last night. One of them must be watching the building, like Bubba said. Saw me leave with Aiden, then either followed us or called his accomplice to toy with me."

Gray agreed that the possible scenarios were more easily explained by a team of stalkers. That was already a departure from the story Allie had told him about how Boggs had thought he was such hot spit that he didn't need anyone's help, and gave credence to Bubba's claim that this might be about him as much as it was Allie. "Did you get a description of either driver?"

Aiden snorted at the question. "Nothing usable. Black. White. Latino. Skinny. Stocky. Ball cap. Team logo. No logo. No ball cap. The only thing they agreed on was that the driver of the wrecked car was a man. You would think with all the costumes around here, a regular Joe would stand out."

"Where eyewitnesses fail, forensic evidence steps in and tells us the truth." Lexi came up beside Aiden and rested her hand on Blue's head. "Go. Let us work the scene, see what answers we can find here." Then she reached for Allie's hand and grinned. "Are we still on for an afternoon of cleaning and painting?"

Gray was thinking more along the lines of taking Allie home and locking her up in his apartment with an armed guard outside.

But Allie *did* have that stubborn streak. "You guys still want to help me?"

"You're important to Malone, so that means you're important to us." Lexi winked. "Besides, Chelsea found this miracle cleaning solution online that she's brewing on her stove. Guaranteed to get bloodstains out. She's anxious to try it."

"Brewing on her stove? Is it going to disintegrate my walls?"

Everyone but Gray and Jackson laughed as Shane explained the way Chelsea's mind and big heart worked. "That's our Chelsea. Smartest one in the room, but she marches to the beat of her own drum. If she's determined to help someone, you can't stop her."

"Well, I wouldn't want to hurt her feelings," Allie teased, understanding their appreciation for the most unique member of their team. "All right. Yes. Thank you. You all come on over whenever you're ready. I'll have food and drinks for everyone." After each of them said their goodbyes and moved on to get their crime scene kits and start gathering evidence, Allie turned to Gray. "I need to get to the clinic. I told Maeve I'd work for her this morning. The clinic is busy on Saturdays, and they'll be short-staffed if I don't show up. I'll need to stop at the store on the way home."

"Someone just tried to kill you." The locked apartment and armed guard were sounding better and better to Gray.

"I don't think so. I'm following your lead and trying to stick to rational thinking. If he wanted me dead, why not shoot me? Why not run me down when I was crossing the street? Why play that cat and mouse game?" She held up the picture on her phone again. "Why leave me this?"

Gray settled his hand at her back and turned toward his van. "I'll take you back to my place to relax."

Allie quickly stepped in front of him, stopping him. "I won't sleep. I need to stay busy. Plus, I gave Maeve my word."

"All right. I'll go with you."

She splayed her fingers at the center of his chest, and he automatically pulled his shoulders back the way he did when they were working together at the clinic. "No, you won't. You're needed here. Find the answer, Gray. Make this stop. I want to have a regular date with you that doesn't involve me freaking out or either one of us looking over our shoulder."

"A real date, huh?" He leaned into the heat of her hand.

"Yeah, stud. So, get to work. I'll have Aiden ask one of the traffic officers to drive me to the clinic. I've got a spare set of scrubs I can change into there. Then you can pick me up when you're done here. You must be feeling more confident with your driving if you got through convention traffic okay."

"I'll be there." When she started to leave, he caught

her hand and curled his fingers around her waist, the way he did when they were dancing for therapy. But he kept right on pulling until her hips butted against his and he could lean in and capture her lips in a kiss. Her mouth softened under his and clung, long enough for him to remember they had an audience. But he didn't care. He didn't think he would ever get his fill of kissing Allie. And he couldn't stand the thought of anyone taking that opportunity away from him. The old Gray reared up in him, making a promise. "This guy doesn't get to win. Be safe, babe. I want that date, too."

ALLIE'S APARTMENT WAS a whole new shade of beige by the time Gray stretched out in bed and stared up at the ceiling. He'd put on a favorite old boot camp T-shirt and his sleep shorts. A hot shower had eased the ache in his muscles. And a quick massage of therapeutic lotion into his thighs had eased the chafing of wearing his prosthetic legs for several hours longer than he was accustomed to. He'd been well compensated for all the painting he'd done, with several slices of pizza, a cold beer, and the relief of watching Allie's trepidation about being back in her apartment, surrounded by that hateful word, turn into smiles and joking with his friends.

Chelsea's miracle cleaner had done the trick and removed the blood, although it had also ruined the finish on the cabinets above Allie's kitchen peninsula. Allie figured Bubba Summerfield should be called in to do at least some of the work he was paid to do. And Gray figured he'd make sure he was on hand and Allie was out with friends or at work while the super who kept eyeballing her and making her uncomfortable was in her apartment making the repairs. Maybe he'd ask Aiden if he could borrow Blue for a visit that day, too. Since Bubba had claimed to be intimidated by the K-9, Blue's presence might make him work faster.

If he had the energy, Gray would have grinned into the darkness at the idea.

He'd been up early to make sure Allie got off safely for her run. Then Aiden had called with the news of Allie being pursued and the subsequent crash. Gray didn't think driving the modified van was going to be an issue for him anymore since he'd proved on two occasions now that he could drive it fast and get to Allie when she needed him. Or maybe a truer statement was when he needed to see her.

After that, he'd worked the crime scene with his team and then gone back to the lab to type the blood samples he'd taken from the car, and to spend some time on the phone with the commandant at NAVCONBRIG CHASN. The commandant had been especially interested in the idea that one of his prisoners could send a personal item to someone in Kansas City or give it to a visitor there. Although there was no evidence of outgoing mail from Boggs, they couldn't rule out that he'd arranged something with one of his visitors. Gray had requested photographs of all of Boggs's visitors over the past few months, and the commandant had agreed to pull shots from the video in the visitation room and email them to Gray Monday morning. Then he'd picked up Allie at the clinic—thankfully with no drama there, with Friesen off duty and no unwanted gifts showing up. Gray had then spent the afternoon priming and the evening painting.

His body was exhausted, but his brain couldn't seem to shut down. He felt cold in his apartment tonight. The bed was too soft. It was too quiet, lying here by himself. It was surprising how quickly he'd become addicted to having Allie beside him. But she insisted she needed to stay at her own place tonight. If she didn't face her demons on her own, she might not ever be able to. Gray thought that was a load of manure—Allie Tate could face down any enemy and come out on top as long as she believed she could. So, with an invitation to come over for breakfast, he'd come back to his own apartment. Let independent Allie have her space. Let her solidify her strength in the way she needed to. Let her go.

Even for one night, it was the hardest thing Gray had ever had to do.

He missed her. The jolt of her cold hands in his. The soft sounds of her breathing as she slept. The uninhibited way she coiled her body around his.

Although they'd shared as many deep, sometimes troubling, discussions, they'd shared just as many light and trivial conversations. Her parents lived in the small town of Fulton, Missouri. Her favorite color was pink. And she couldn't stand to watch horror movies. She'd trained as a medic and had served aboard an aircraft carrier before specializing in physical therapy and getting reassigned to Jacksonville. She'd survived Noah Boggs's campaign to terrorize and discredit her, testifying in front of an Admiral's Mast, and an attempt on her life.

And she made Gray feel more like a man than he'd felt since that last minute before the RPG had hit. She made him feel strong, necessary, normal.

But if her need for him was just about this case, just about keeping her grounded and warm until this guy was identified…

He heard the soft knock in the hallway outside the apartment. Gray shut down his thoughts and tuned in to the sound. The noise was so quiet that it could have been someone knocking at another apartment door. Allie's? Gray sat up, as alert as he'd been on a nighttime patrol over in the Middle East. As underhanded as this stalker had been, would he really knock on her door in the middle of the night and announce himself? This guy was about stealth and surprise, not, "Hey, I'm here. Let me in."

When someone knocked again, he realized it was his own door. Gray could think of only one person who'd be paying him a visit. He pulled his chair to the edge of the bed and swung himself onto the seat. He heard Allie's voice calling to him as he wheeled his way through the apartment.

"Gray?"

He unlatched the dead bolt and turned the knob before she could knock again. She startled when the door swung open, and she retreated half a step.

"Were you asleep?" she asked, hugging her arms around her waist.

"No."

"I can't sleep, either." Gray held out his hand and she followed him into the apartment, keeping hold of him while he shut and bolted the door. Then she did the damnedest, most beautiful thing and sat on his lap. She turned sideways across his thighs and hugged her legs up toward her chest. "It's amazing how fast I've gotten used to you holding me in your arms. Besides…paint fumes."

If he was meant to laugh, he didn't. Instead, he wound his arms around her and pulled her to him. He buried his nose in the honey-colored waterfall of her unbound hair and inhaled its freshly washed scent. "Such beautiful hair," he murmured before kissing her temple. "So beautiful," he whispered against her mouth before claiming her lips and worshipping them.

Her lips parted and their tongues battled for supremacy as they stroked and tasted each other. She tasted of minty toothpaste and smelled like flowers. Gray closed his teeth gently around the swollen curve of her bottom lip and she moaned. He felt the vibrations of that sexy sound humming through his blood and feeding that most male part of his anatomy.

"Are you safe?" he managed to ask when he came up for air. "Has anything happened? Are you hurt?"

"I'm fine. The demons…" Her breathing sounded as ragged as his. "I want to stay with you, Gray. Please let me stay. I need you."

"All of me?" he asked. His body was desperate to have hers, but his brain needed to hear her say the words.

"Yes."

Thrilling to the surge of power her demand gave him, Gray anchored Allie's arms behind his neck and freed his hands to push them into the bedroom. This felt right, inevitable, maybe, to have her here in his space again—to feel her hip pressed against his groin, to absorb her heat and scent, to hold her, to love her, to be with her.

When he reached the bed, he lifted her in his arms and tossed her on top of the covers. He pushed himself up and spider-walked to the center of the bed where she was kicking off her slippers and unzipping the hoodie he'd lent her. He crawled over her, stretching out until her breasts were pillowed beneath his chest, her sharp nipples goading him to taste them through the thin cotton of her T-shirt. She gasped as he closed his mouth over a turgid peak and swirled his tongue around the sensitive nub. With the material wet and clinging to the dimple of her areola, he plumped the taut, responsive mound and sucked her into his mouth.

"Gray!" She bucked beneath him, calling his name on a strangled gasp of pleasure.

When he turned his attention to the other breast, she clasped the back of his head and held his mouth to her, even as she writhed beneath him, letting his hard body get intimately acquainted with every soft curve of hers. She ran her hands down along his flanks and swept them back up beneath his shirt.

"I want to touch you," she begged, pressing a kiss to his pectoral muscle, then groaning in frustration when the shirt caught beneath his arms.

Chuckling against her tender breast, Gray did a push-up to give her the space she needed to whisk the shirt off over his head. But the angle pushed his hips into hers and his thigh jammed against the damp heat of her pajama pants. Allie whimpered and Gray immediately rocked back onto his stumps on either side of her thighs. "I'm sorry." His face burned as his body cooled. "Did I hurt you?"

"What? No, I—"

"I don't know exactly how to do this." Damn. Now he looked like a giant spider hovering over her. He swung his leg over her and sat beside her on the bed. Frustrated and embarrassed and angry at himself for forgetting his limitations, Gray raked his fingers through his short hair. "I've haven't done this since..."

She sat up facing him, her eyes narrowed in concern, her hair falling in wild disarray around her shoulders. "Gray, tell me exactly what's wrong. You didn't hurt me. You hit the money spot with your leg, and your weight plus the pressure building inside me shocked me with a zing of pleasure."

"A zing?" He shook his head. "Then that was a lucky shot. I don't know how to balance myself so I don't crush you. There's no sensation in the ends on my legs so I can't tell if I'm zinging or hurting you. I used to do this without thinking. I want you so much, but I'm not sure I can make this good for you."

"Not good?" He shouldn't have been surprised when Allie tugged on his thigh, turning him slightly before she crawled onto his lap. She curled her legs around his hips, settling herself right against his swollen member. His legs might not be working, but that part of his body was all too aware of her heat nestling against him. "Oh, I don't know. You kissed me senseless, then you carried me to the bedroom." While she talked, she shrugged out of the hoodie and pulled the damp T-shirt over her head so that they were both topless as she guided his hands to her waist.

"How romantic," he scoffed. "I was in the damn chair—"

"I did not walk." She wound her arms around his neck and pulled herself closer until those button-tipped breasts branded his chest. She rubbed them against him, as if she enjoyed the sensation of friction as much as he did. "I'm not a petite, delicate flower of femininity, Gray. But you hauled me into your lap like I was a delicate little thing. You tossed me onto the bed and were on me before I even stopped bouncing. All impulsive, needy, Neanderthalic turn-ons for me." She dragged her fingers down his chest and teased the flat of his stomach where it met the waistband of his shorts. Gray sucked in a breath and his fingers clenched at her waist. Oh, he was so far gone with this strong, beautiful woman. "And you want me, Gray. Hopefully, half as much as I want you right now."

"But I want it to be good for you."

She hooked her fingers into the material of his shorts and tugged them down. "Is that for me?" Gray leaned his forehead against hers and groaned as she wrapped her hand around him. "Then it'll be good. Do you have a condom?"

Gray growled and nodded before reaching past her into the nightstand. He pulled out an unopened box and handed it to her.

Her eyes widened. "Well, that's a lot of pressure to go through all of these in one night."

He snorted a laugh at her wry comment. Bless this woman. She was putting him at ease and turning him on at the same time. She'd coached and prodded and laughed with him and stood her ground to get him to walk again—to teach him to dance on his new legs.

She was doing the same now and he loved her for it. He tunneled his fingers into her hair and showed her how grateful he was with his kiss.

Her skin was flushed from her cheeks to her breasts, and they were both breathing hard by the time he pulled away.

"Let's start with one." Allie's fingers shook as she opened the box and ripped open a package. "Okay, now I'm a little nervous."

Gray chuckled and took the condom from her. "Big man, big business."

She laughed as he rolled it on. "Totally Neanderthalic turn-on."

"Is Neanderthalic even a word?" he teased. He could do this for her, for them.

"Gray, I haven't been with a man since before Noah. And, obviously, I don't have good memories there."

"Then we'll make new ones. Good ones."

She wound her arms around his neck and kissed the corner of his mouth. "I'd like that. I'd really, really like that."

"I've noticed that you still have clothes on," he pointed out. With a flurry of bumping hands and stolen kisses and shared laughter, he helped her to her feet so she could shed her pajama pants. "I want you more than my next breath, Allison Tate. But I still need to figure out how all this is going to work. Will you be patient with me?"

Holding his hand for balance, she climbed back

onto the bed and straddled his lap, fitting her slick heat against him. "No."

She pressed her finger to his lips, silencing his protest and helping him understand her answer meant she wanted him as badly as he wanted her.

"We have desire. We have trust. Everything else will fall into place."

Later, when they were sated with each other's bodies and Allie was sleeping securely in his arms, Gray felt as if everything he'd ever wanted for his new civilian life had indeed fallen into place.

And he wasn't going to let some cowardly, obsessed stalker and his mind games take it from him.

Chapter Thirteen

"Anything new?" Mac Taylor asked, catching Gray skimming through the information packet that had just been delivered from Colonel Martin Wilcox in Charleston, South Carolina.

The Monday morning staff meeting was one of the few times during the week that the entire team of criminalists and lab techs got together to discuss progress on ongoing investigations, reassess case assignments, check where help might be needed and map out priorities for the team. Gray had jotted down a note on a shooting where he needed to analyze the blood spatter and determine if the wound had been accidentally self-inflicted or was the result of a drunken brawl that had gotten out of hand. But beyond that, he had spent most of the meeting with his mind on the weekend he'd spent with Allie and reading the colonel's report on Noah Boggs's recent activities.

They'd spent a good portion of Saturday night and Sunday morning in his bed, making love and discussing future plans, including the decision that she would be moving in with him for the time being. Yesterday afternoon, they'd gone next door to her apartment and packed some clothes that were now hanging in his closet and folded up in his drawers, along with the flower-scented shampoo and shower gel that were sitting in his shower. The plan was to live together until "Payback" was identified and put away—both for Allie's sense of mental and emotional security and his own. And after that? He was still working up the courage to lay his heart on the line again. Gray had no doubt that he was in love with Allie Tate, and would get down on whatever legs he had left and propose to her. But the idea that history might repeat itself made him cautious about giving any more of himself. The man he was now hadn't been enough for Brittany in the long run. What if it turned out that he was the man Allie needed now, while they weathered this crisis together—but when she was free and able to cope on her own again, she'd be thanking him for the good times and moving on.

But great sex and Allie moving into his place probably wasn't the *new* that Mac wanted him to report on.

Gray included everyone seated around the conference table and leaning against the wall behind the table in his report. "Colonel Wilcox has isolated Boggs in the brig until he can determine if and how the prisoner smuggled his keychain out. There is a picture here from Boggs's personal effects that confirms that the keys Allie found in the black car were his." He held up the envelope and another file folder that he wanted to compare to the visitors' log the colonel had sent. "Other than his attorney and a distant cousin of some kind, all of Boggs's visitors have been women. Wilcox thinks he might have some kind of pen pal fan club going on."

"Ew," Chelsea piped up from her laptop and the far end of the table. "I never understood how that was a thing. I've known several guys who have gone to prison. And nothing about them makes me want to marry them or even write them."

There were chuckles around the room before Mac spoke again. "What about the blood in the black car Saturday morning. You'll be processing that today?"

"Yes, sir." Gray shared an affinity for the crime lab boss and a great deal of respect. Mac was also a disabled criminalist, having been blinded in one eye in an explosion several years ago. Despite his handicap, he'd worked his way up through the ranks of the KCPD Crime Lab, from its old location to this new facility. He'd married and had a family. Gray hoped to be running his own lab and raising his own family one day. "I can already tell you that the blood I processed came from the perp hitting his head when the vehicle crashed. The airbag created a serious head injury, but KCPD should be looking for a guy with a couple of black eyes from a broken nose, or one who has stitches in his forehead."

Aiden Murphy added his two cents to the report. "The car had stolen plates, and the VIN number had been etched off, probably with acid. I'm guessing it came from a chop shop, so nobody's going to be reporting it stolen."

Mac made a note. "So, that's a dead end." He gave out some secondary assignments related to Allie's case. "Jackson, you follow up on Boggs's cousin, see if there's any way he could be our guy. Chelsea, I want to ID all those pen pals who've been to see him."

"Yes, sir."

Mac had one more question for Gray. "What about any leads from the Kleinschmidt case? Do you think Allie is being used as a means to target you?"

Gray shrugged. "A couple of things are pointing that way. But I've got no hard facts to confirm it yet. Just a creepy building super and a bloodstained note."

"Stay on it. I liked Allie when I met her Saturday at her apartment. I think she's good for you. Let's keep her safe."

"Thank you, sir. That's the plan."

Mac moved on to the next agenda item, and Gray returned to his lab after the meeting was dismissed a short time later.

He was on his third mug of coffee, gleaning through the file of names Chelsea had dropped off a few minutes earlier. Noah Boggs's pen pals were a varied lot of five women—blonde, brunette, turquoise hair; two of them young with drugs and prostitution on their record; one a spinsterly, lonely heart who was looking for a connection wherever she could get it; and one older woman with snow-white hair. The grainy image from the camera didn't offer a straight look at her face, but the woman looked old enough to be his mother.

Gray shook his head as his disgust for Noah Boggs grew. That man was a player who was used to getting what he wanted, and who wasn't above using anyone who could help him reach his goal—or hurting anyone who tried to keep him from it.

He spread the files from NAVCONBRIG CHASN out across his desk and pulled up the Jamie Kleinschmidt file on his computer. He'd pored over every bit of information available to him from Charleston, South Carolina, and here in Kansas City, Missouri. He wished the answer he needed was as easy to analyze as a drop of blood under a microscope. But it was proving to be as difficult as losing his legs and his buddies and learning how to walk and trust again.

Since blood was his field of expertise, maybe he should go back to comparing the samples he'd taken from Allie's apartment to the victim samples Kleinschmidt had stored in his basement. Hell, maybe he should cross-match blood types and see if any of them were B-positive or B-negative. Maybe that explained the connection to Allie's key ring.

Wait. B-positive?

Gray sat up straight in his chair as the germ of an answer toyed with the fringes of his memory. He shuffled some papers and scrolled through the file on his screen until he had nothing but biographical data on display.

Jamie Kleinschmidt had B-positive blood.

The man listed as his father did not.

His mother was B-positive.

"His mother…"

Gray scanned the images from the courtroom from Kleinschmidt's trial. In all the days he'd reported to the witness stand, he'd never seen a father or mother. It had always been Kleinschmidt alone with his attorneys on one side of the courtroom, and the DA and the parents and families and friends of Kleinschmidt's victims on the other. Kleinschmidt had a sister, but apparently, she'd disowned him when he was arrested. She'd never showed up in the courtroom, either.

"B-positive…" *Think, Malone.*

He looked back at the pictures of the women who'd visited Boggs in prison. One of them could be Kleinschmidt's sister. Could the cousin be the accomplice?

"B…"

Gray swore.

The answer had been staring at him the whole time. Part of it, anyway. And it had never even registered. Well, it registered now.

Hurting Allie was all about hurting *him*. *He* was

the *Payback* Allie's stalker and accomplice wanted. Yes, they were using the same tactics Noah Boggs had used against her to keep her from testifying against him. But this wasn't about Boggs at all. He was the tool, but her stalker was the one wielding the information he must have provided.

Boggs wasn't playing those women. One of them was playing him.

There it was in black-and-white at the very top of the file.

Payback for a disturbed young man who'd killed himself after Gray's testimony had sent him to prison.

Jamie *Burroughs* Kleinschmidt.

Nothing was more dangerous than a mother protecting her young.

Unless it was a mother taking vengeance on the man she blamed for her child's death.

GRAY STUMBLED OUT of the lab, catching his right crutch and dropping his phone. He'd only gotten off one text to Allie before his legs started itching with the need to move. To take action. To get to her before it was too late.

Where are you?

By the time he picked up his phone, she'd answered.

At work.

What patient are you working with?

He'd picked up an audience by the time he'd typed in the next message. Jackson and Mac were strolling out of the lounge with fresh mugs of coffee in their hands. Their posture changed from relaxed to intense in a heartbeat when they saw how Gray was trotting down the hall in his uneven gait. Damn it. He should have looked into those running blade prostheses Allie had told him about. How was he supposed to get to her fast enough when her life could be in danger this very minute?

Jackson handed his mug off to Mac and cupped Gray's elbow to balance him. All three men moved at a faster pace. "Figure it out?" Jackson asked.

Gray nodded as he read Allie's reply.

What's going on? Is something wrong? Did you match the blood to someone? Is that Noah's key ring?

He handed his crutches off to Jackson and leaned on his friend's strength to free his hands to type.

Get into the locker room and lock yourself in. Tell Hunter I'm sending the police and he needs to guard that door with his life.

"Don't have the accomplice yet, but it's related to the Kleinschmidt case."

Okay, now you're just pissing me off. You're scaring me, and I don't need that. What is going on? You obviously think I'm in danger. I'm not going to save myself and leave my patients and coworkers to face whatever is happening.

Ivy Burroughs.

Gray said the name out loud as he typed.

"Snooty old lady at the clinic?" Jackson confirmed.

Mac shook his head. "An old lady is behind this?"

"Maybe not so old," Gray explained. "And maybe that's why she has the accomplice."

What about her?

Is she there?

Yes. She's working with Maeve.

"Damn it. The perp is with her right now." Gray tried to run.

A minute passed before the next message hit.

GRAYSON MALONE, TALK TO ME!

Ivy is Jamie Kleinschmidt's mother. I didn't remember her because she was never at the trial. I didn't meet her until PT.

Mrs. B is the widow of an Army colonel.

"Am I driving, or are you?" Jackson asked as they neared the exit.

"Take the CSIU van," Mac ordered, meaning Jackson was at the wheel. "It'll get you through morning traffic faster. If that woman is there, you can process her from head to toe. I'll notify Brian Stockman. You want police backup?"

"Yes."

"In the meantime, I'll get a search warrant and send Lexi and the rest of the team to Ivy Burroughs's address. See if we can find links to the blood, the gifts or either of you two."

Jackson set Gray's crutches inside the cab of the crime scene van and offered his shoulder for Gray to boost himself up into the passenger seat. "Thank you, sir." He kept typing, knowing Allie wouldn't answer a phone if she was with a patient.

Her husband was a grunt who was killed in Desert Storm. She reinvented her history before coming to the clinic. Hell, she probably doesn't even limp. She could have gone to a doctor and faked the symptoms to get prescribed PT just to get closer to me. To find out what I care about. How to hurt me.

Yeah. Hurting Allie definitely cut him deep with guilt and pain.

Why wouldn't she be at the trial supporting her son?

Unless she disowned him for killing those women? But then why seek vengeance for his death?

Jackson swung the van out of the parking lot and turned on the siren as Gray recalled the information Chelsea had compiled for him.

She was in the hospital during the trial. Are you locked inside the room yet?

She feels guilty for not supporting him when he needed her. Then he kills himself and she thinks this is how to redeem her motherhood badge. By taking care of her son's needs after his death. Better late than never?

Now she wanted to play psychologist? The why's didn't matter. Ivy's note had promised that payback would be coming soon. He needed Allie to get to safety.

She was in a mental hospital.

OMG.

Now she understood the urgency of the situation.

Yeah. Just lock yourself in.

I don't see Ben. Or Doug.

Still have no clue who's helping Ivy. But it has to be someone with access to you. Watch your six.

Several seconds passed without any reply.

Allie?

Lieutenant?

Talk to me.

The next message came from someone else.

Go home, Mr. Malone. She's mine now.

Chapter Fourteen

The power was out at physical therapy and chaos reigned supreme when Gray and Jackson pulled up.

Traffic had been barricaded off at the end of the block in either direction. There were two fire engines from Station 13 and an ambulance parked in front of the building. Although he didn't see any hoses leading into the building, or any ladders extended, there were plenty of firefighters moving in and out of the place. Gray got a sick feeling in the pit of his stomach when he saw a woman wrapped in a blanket, sitting on the bumper of the ambulance. "Son of a bitch." The van was still rocking to a stop as he pushed open the door. "Allie?"

He recognized some of the patients and staff gathered across the street at the entrance to the parking garage. But he didn't stop to check on any of them. He made a beeline for the ambulance when Ben Hunter stepped away from the police officer he'd been talking to and put up his good hand to stop him. "It's not her."

Gray exhaled a sigh of relief and took a moment to survey their surroundings. Jackson showed up beside him with his crutches, enabling him to move more securely on his own. He recognized the officer Ben had been talking to, Gina Cutler.

"Officer." Gray acknowledged her, but kept searching the crowd for a tall woman with a honey-blond ponytail.

"Mr. Malone."

"When I called it in, they said Cutler was already working the case," Ben explained.

Gray's gaze went back to Ben. "Then where is Allie?"

"Not here."

Gray leaned toward the shorter man. "What do you mean she's not here? You're supposed to be keeping an eye on her."

"I know, man. I dropped the ball. I was sitting in the lobby, reading a book, when the lights went out. I immediately went back to try and find her, but folks were panicking. I pulled the fire alarm to get everyone moving toward the exit and I waited for her to come out." Ben tugged on his beard. "But she never did. I went in to look once things were clear, but the firefighters arrived and ordered me out, too."

"You told them she was unaccounted for? They searched for her, too?"

Ben nodded. "They said a circuit breaker had been thrown. It was no power outage."

Ben looked appropriately contrite, but Gray wasn't

ready to give up his anger yet. "Anyone else unaccounted for?"

"I don't know. I was only paying attention to your woman. I saw her when she started her latest therapy session. Then she was having a texting conversation—"

"That was me."

"—Then the lights went out and she was gone."

And Gray had no idea where Ivy and her accomplice had taken her.

"Where's Ivy Burroughs?" He swiveled his gaze from Ben to Gina Cutler and back, demanding answers. "She's Jamie Kleinschmidt's mother. Possibly mentally unstable. She's got an ax to grind with me."

"Kleinschmidt the serial killer?" Gina's dark eyes widened, and she pulled out her notebook.

"Yeah."

"She blames you for her son's death in prison?"

Gray nodded. "The messages? Following Allie? She got that info from Allie's ex—probably the only way you can knock that woman down is to put her through the mind games he played on her again. But the blood is about me. My blood evidence is what got Kleinschmidt convicted." He fisted his hand and tapped the top of Gina's notebook, willing her to understand how desperate he was. "She's going to hurt Allie. She's going to drain her blood or something equally horrible to get to me. To punish me. I have to find her before that happens."

"You don't think Allie could take down that little

old biddy?" Ben apologized to Gina or whoever he thought he'd offended. "There's no way that witch could have dragged Allie out of here. Even if Allie was drugged or knocked out, she couldn't move the body."

Jackson explained in his shorthand way. "Accomplice."

"Who?" Gina Cutler asked, taking down notes.

"Some guy with a broken nose or fresh cut on his head." Gray turned to Ben, checking for bruising on his face and on every other man who walked past them. "You haven't seen anybody like that around here, have you?"

Ben shook his head. "I've lost my edge. I've been out of the game too long."

Officer Cutler closed her notebook. "I'll put a BOLO out for Allie and Mrs. Burroughs. I'll send someone to her home address right now."

"A CSI team is already en route," Jackson reported.

Home?

Go home, Mr. Malone. She's mine now.

Jackson knew how to read his friend. "Something just popped into that head of yours." Gray nodded, backing toward the van. "Where you going?"

"Keys in the ignition?"

"Malone? You can't drive that van."

"Then you're driving."

"Where?"

Gray pointed back to Ben. "As soon as KCFD clears

the scene, I want you to go back inside and search again. Open every locker, every storage cabinet. Look under every bed and table. If it can help us find Allie or convict Ivy, I want it in our lab."

"Mr. Hunter is not a member of KCPD or the crime lab," Gina pointed out.

"Then you stay with him and make sure anything he does is legit."

"Where are you going, Malone?" Gina demanded. "What aren't you telling me?" She grabbed Gray's arm to stop him climbing into the van. "These people may be killers. You need backup."

Gray pulled his shoulders back and centered his balance over his hips. "I'm a United States Marine, Officer. I *am* the backup."

ALLIE'S CHIN BOBBED against her chest and she snapped it back, fighting to stay awake despite the headache pounding through the fog in her brain. Her arms and legs felt like they were trapped in a vat of gelatin. She squeezed her fingers into fists, trying to regain the feeling there, and she wondered why she couldn't raise her arms to pull free the strands of hair that were caught in the corner of her mouth.

She blinked her eyes open, struggling to bring the world into focus, sensing that it was utterly important that she know where she was. She heard the jangling of metal clinking together before she saw a woman's head with dark hair with the striking white stripe of a birthmark running through the perfectly coiffed style.

And then a burning hot poker pierced the back of her right calf and Allie screamed. Only, the sound seemed to reverberate in her ears and stuff up her nose.

"Like that?" a man's voice asked from behind her. "There's not much blood. Can't I go higher?"

"No." A woman's sharp voice answered from the direction of the white stripe. "That and the arms are enough for now. Much higher and you'll nick the femoral artery and she'll bleed out before the show's over."

The red-hot poker stabbed into her left calf and Allie whimpered. She realized now that the man was cutting her. Nothing like inflicting some of the worst pain of her life to jolt her senses awake and rouse her from the stupor of whatever drug they'd given her.

Allie had been in an alarming conversation with Gray, hurrying toward the safety of the one door in the clinic she could lock, scanning every table and treatment room for Ivy Burroughs. She'd pushed open the door to the staff locker room and quickly checked the bathrooms and run her hand along all the locker doors to make sure they were empty. She'd turned back to the door to see Ivy standing there.

Faking a smile, Allie greeted her. "Hey, Mrs. Burroughs. This is a restricted area. Did you lose track of Maeve?"

The older woman smiled. That was when she realized Ivy Burroughs wasn't as old as she pretended to be. She wasn't limping, either.

Then the lights had gone out, she'd felt a sharp prick in her neck, and she was waking up here.

Ivy Burroughs was stalking her, copying the nightmare of her relationship with Noah. But why? What had she ever done to this woman beyond trying to help her heal from her hip injury, which apparently wasn't a real injury, at all? And who the hell was the man behind her who seemed to be taking such pleasure in swiping his fingers through the blood trickling down the back of her leg, then smearing it up to her bottom, then all the way back down her leg.

Alarmed for a moment that she was completely vulnerable to these people, Allie looked down and inhaled a breath of relief through her clogged-up nose to see that she was wearing her bra and panties. Sad to say, she wore nothing else. And even as she thought of how cold it was here, a sea of goose bumps erupted across her skin, and she shivered violently. Shaking herself awake.

Stay busy. Don't think. Don't feel. Just get through tonight. Don't let him get into your head and take anything else from you. You can fight again tomorrow.

The mantra gave her some comfort simply because it reminded her that she was a survivor. Although she had a very scary feeling that if she didn't get busy and figure out how to get away from this couple right now, she might not have a tomorrow.

With her head still downcast, she opened her eyes

and saw her toes dangling above a spotted tarp on the floor beneath her. Red spots. Blood drops. Her blood. She raised her gaze to the kitchen cabinets. Her kitchen cabinets that had been defaced by these two, and thoroughly cleaned by true friends just this past week. There was a row of empty glass baby jars lined across the counter.

She was hanging from the ceiling fan in her kitchen, hanging by her arms. Bubba had made a point of bragging about his handiwork, how that fan could hold a side of beef because he'd double-anchored it to the crossbeam that ran across the ceiling. She'd thought it a weird, uncomfortable conversation at the time. Now she was the side of beef! Still weird. Still uncomfortable.

Still bleeding.

Oh, my God. Gray! They were doing this to hurt Gray.

Not that she was feeling real whippy at the moment herself. This was all related to that serial murder case Gray had talked about. They were going to fill those jars with her blood. Then what? Throw them at him? Ruin one of his investigations? Torture him with them somehow? Were they going to drain his blood, too?

Gray! Where are you? You said you had my six. Come find me, Marine.

No. Don't come. They want to hurt you. Stay away!

Her man had known such pain already. Too much pain for him to bear alone.

She wanted to be his helpmate. His partner. His friend. His lover. His wife.

When he was ready.

Oh, she was so ready to take on the grumpy Marine.

To teach him his value. To show him her need.

I love you, Grayson Malone.

Believe that you are loved.

That you are whole. That you are perfect.

That you are mine.

Allie felt something take root inside her, something warm and powerful that seeped into every frightened neuron and spread through her veins, clearing her fuzzy brain and giving her a fire these two pretenders could never take from her.

"She's awake." Ivy Burroughs sounded pleased, as if whatever sick game she was playing could now continue.

Somehow, the feral scream Allie roared inside her head had been heard. Or her posture had changed with her newfound resolve. Or she was just putting off that don't-mess-with-me vibe that she'd learned in her Navy self-defense classes.

And if Bubba Summerfield put his hand on her butt one more time…

Allie twisted her body around, glaring down at Bubba's matching black eyes. He must have broken his nose in the car crash in the alleyway. Her accusatory words came out as a growl, and he laughed at her inability to communicate. "Can I stick her now?"

He grabbed her hips and spun her back around, the sudden centrifugal motion tearing through her arms and making her dizzy. He drew the dull edge of the knife across the back of her thighs. It wasn't sharp enough to cut, but she felt the cold metal burn her skin as if he had drawn blood. "I'm going to stick you for every time you smacked my hand away. Every time you told me off with one of those clever lines you thought were so funny. Every time I told you I was interested, and you shot me down."

"She loves the cripple, James," Ivy explained, her bracelets jangling as she held her hand out for the knife. It was odd to hear Bubba called by his given name. But then, Allie couldn't imagine the haughty older woman even uttering the word *Bubba.* "That's the only way this could work. I needed to find out what Mr. Malone loved so that I could take it from him. The same way he took my son from me."

She rested the blade against Allie's sternum and pushed until Allie felt the skin split open. She whimpered at the pain, but refused to look away from the madness in Ivy's eyes. She'd thought the woman was pushy, eccentric, self-entitled. Instead, she'd been pushing her and Gray together, prepping her like a lamb to slaughter. She must have talked to Noah, discovered what scared her most and proceeded to carry those acts out to make her turn to Gray for help and comfort, and trigger his protective instincts.

"He's going to figure out that message you sent

him, Ivy," Bubba whined. "Let's finish the job, get my money and satisfaction, and get out of here."

Ivy set the knife on the counter and made herself at home in a chair that was going straight to the dumpster when all this was done—if Allie survived. "Not yet. I want to be here to watch Mr. Malone break the same way he broke my son when he sent him to prison. Jamie was too fragile for incarceration." A serial killer? Fragile? Really? Oh, if this gag was gone and her snark could come out. "I couldn't be there for him during the trial to hire a better lawyer and keep him out of prison. But I'm here for him now. I'm making things right." She tilted her scarily calm eyes up to Allie. "You know, dear, this was never personal. I believe I might have liked you under different circumstances. But I could see you had caught Malone's eye. That made you expendable." She crossed her arms in a jangle of bracelets. "I really did like those electric heat pulse treatments you put on my hip. I'll miss those."

Big. Fat. Whup.

"Come on, Ivy," Bubba whined. "I don't intend to be here when the cops come." He picked up the knife. "You can stay and watch the show if that gives you the satisfaction you need. But I'm cutting her and getting out now."

"You'll do no such thing." Ivy leaped from the chair, older maybe, but certainly not infirm. She wrapped her hand around Bubba's on the knife and a struggle ensued. Allie was fairly certain this wasn't a good development for her. Their grip on the knife loosened and the knife flew past her stomach. Allie sucked in her breath to avoid the blade.

"What is this, some kind of suicide mission for you, lady? I'm not going to prison."

"You work for me, young man. My son would never disobey me like this."

Bubba stumbled against Allie, knocking her into motion like a pendulum. "I'm not your son, you stupid old woman."

Allie bumped into Bubba and started spinning. She heard the slap of Ivy's palm across the man's cheek. "How dare you speak to me like that!"

Feeling nauseous, Allie tried to spot anything she could latch on to so she could stop her spinning. When she swung into Bubba again, she knew.

"Allie!"

Gray!

She screamed his name behind her gag as a heavy, metal ramrod splintered through her door and knocked it open.

The crash was enough of a distraction for Allie to pull her long, strong runner's legs up and wrap them around Bubba's neck. He clawed at her legs and she squeezed even tighter. Her arms felt like they were coming out of their sockets as he sputtered for breath and started to go limp.

"No!" Bubba's knife clattered to the floor and Ivy scooped it up as police officers swarmed into her apartment. "This isn't how it's supposed to happen. You have to watch her die!"

"Nobody's killing the woman I love!" Gray stumbled into the kitchen in his beautiful rolling gait. In a graceful maneuver any man would have been jealous of, Gray flipped his crutch in his hand, jammed the handle between Ivy's ankles and yanked, flipping her flat on her back.

The knife flew across the kitchen. Stunned by the hard fall, but determined to have her vengeance, Ivy rolled onto her stomach and crawled toward the weapon. "She dies…she destroys you…" Ivy gasped. "Jamie…"

But Gray beat her to the knife and set his immovable prosthetic foot on the blade. "Your son was guilty. And so are you."

As Gina Cutler moved in to handcuff Ivy, Gray turned his attention to Allie.

"I've got this." Two other officers had braced themselves beneath Allie to hold her up and keep her from dislocating both arms or suffocating herself. He wedged his shoulder beneath her bottom to keep her aloft himself. "It's okay, babe, you can let go now. He can't hurt you."

Jim "Bubba" Summerfield was dead weight in the vise of her legs, but she couldn't seem to give up the fight. Allie shook her head. Tears burned her eyes and spilled over as the adrenaline that had given her the strength to survive began to ebb.

"Oh, babe. I'm so sorry. I'm so sorry." His hands

were gentle as they swept the length of her legs, urging her to relax. She couldn't feel the cuts anymore. Oh, hell. She was probably going into shock. Gray noticed. There was rarely any detail about her he missed. "Somebody get that gag off her so she can breathe."

She was vaguely aware of Jackson Dobbs sliding a chair over and climbing up to peel away the tape with a surprising gentleness for his big hands. Her mouth was too dry to spit out the dishcloth stuffed in behind it, so he reached in and pulled it out, dumping both items into an evidence bag that Lexi Callahan-Murphy held out. Lexi quickly sealed the bag and set in on the counter where she labeled it, along with the knife and jars Shane Duvall was packing into his kit.

Allie loved her nerd friends. Supportive and silly and smart. She wasn't alone anymore. Noah hadn't ruined her life.

A tear rolled down her cheek and dripped onto Gray's. She tried to dredge up enough saliva to speak, but her words still came out in a crackly whisper. "I love you, Grayson Malone."

He smiled up at her, the strength of his shoulder never wavering. "I know. I love you, too."

"I know."

His piercing green eyes never left hers as he relayed orders to the people around him. "I want the blanket off the couch, some bolt cutters for that chain up there and this scumbag away from my woman." After a flurry of voices responded with *yes, sir* and *on it*, Gray patted her thigh. "Let go, Lieutenant. I've got your six."

Feeling weak as cooked noodles, Allie allowed her legs to drop away and Bubba sank with a plop to the floor. Her arms screamed with pain as the chain was cut loose and she could lower them into their normal position again. She was surrounded by warmth, shielded by police officers and snug in the sure grip of Gray's arms.

With Jackson at his elbow to steady him, Gray carried her to the gurney waiting out in the hallway. He leaned in to kiss her, and she wished she was strong enough to wrap her arms around him and thoroughly kiss him back. It was over. They were alive.

As the medics stanched a couple of the worst cuts, Allie did find the strength to rub her fingers over his ticklish beard stubble. "You know, one good thing came out of this, Mr. Marine."

"Only one?" He pulled her hand down to warm it between both of his. "What's that?"

"Ivy could see that we meant something to each other even before we admitted it."

"We would have figured it out eventually."

"Yeah, we would have. I'm in love with a very smart man."

"And I'm in love with a very strong woman." He leaned in to kiss the corner of her mouth again. "Thank you for teaching me to dance. And everything else that goes with it."

"Thank you for having my six."

"Always."

When the paramedic scooted Gray aside to inspect another cut, Allie cried out at losing the treasured touch of his hand. "Gray?"

"Yeah, babe." He reappeared above her head, stroking his fingers through her hair, and she smiled.

"How did you know where to find me today? Those two could have taken me anywhere."

"That's easy, Lieutenant. Ivy said I needed to go home. This is the first place that's felt like a home to me for a very long time. And that's because I fell in love with the girl next door."

* * * * *

Look for the final book in USA TODAY *bestselling author Julie Miller's Kansas City Crime Lab miniseries coming soon.*

And if you missed the previous titles in the series, you can find K-9 Patrol *and* Decoding the Truth *now, wherever Harlequin Intrigue books are sold!*

COMING NEXT MONTH FROM

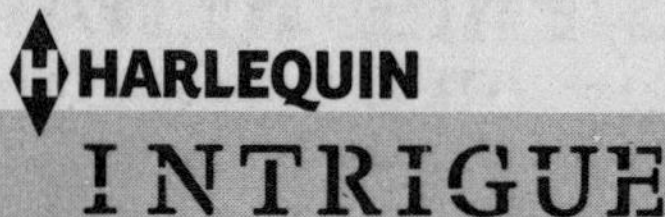

#2157 MAVERICK DETECTIVE DAD

Silver Creek Lawmen: Second Generation • by Delores Fossen

When Detective Noah Ryland and Everly Monroe's tragic pasts make them targets of a vigilante killer, they team up to protect her young daughter and stop the murders. But soon their investigation unleashes a series of vicious attacks...along with reigniting the old heat between them.

#2158 MURDER AT SUNSET ROCK

Lookout Mountain Mysteries • by Debra Webb

A ransacked house suggests that Olivia Ballard's grandfather's death was no mere accident. Deputy Detective Huck Monroe vows to help her uncover the truth. But as dark secrets surrounding Olivia's family are exposed, she'll have to trust the man who broke her heart to stay alive.

#2159 SHROUDED IN THE SMOKIES

A Tennessee Cold Case Story • by Lena Diaz

Former detective Adam Trent is stunned to learn his cold case victim is alive. But Skylar Montgomery is still very much in danger—and desperate for Adam's help. Their investigation leads them to one of Chattanooga's most powerful families...and a vicious web of mystery, intrigue and murder.

#2160 TEXAS BODYGUARD: WESTON

San Antonio Security • by Janie Crouch

Security Specialist Weston Patterson risks everything to keep his charges safe. But protecting wealthy Kayleigh Delacruz is his biggest challenge yet. She doesn't want a bodyguard. But as the kidnapping threat grows, she'll do anything—even trust Weston's expertise—to survive.

#2161 DIGGING DEEPER

by Amanda Stevens

When Thora Graham awakens inside a coffin-like box with no memory of how she got there, Deputy Police Chief Will Dresden, the man she left fifteen years ago, follows the clues to save her life. Their twisted reunion becomes a race against time to stop a serial killer's vengeful scheme.

#2162 K-9 HUNTER

by Cassie Miles

Piper Comstock and her dog, Izzy, live a solitary, peaceful life. Until her best friend is targeted by an assassin. US Marshal Gavin McQueen knows the truth— a witness in protection is compromised. It's dangerous to recruit a civilian to help with the investigation. But is the danger to Piper's life...or Gavin's heart?
